Alice Rose & Sam

a novel by
Kathryn Lasky

HYPERION BOOKS FOR CHILDREN

NEW YORK

First Edition
1 3 5 7 9 10 8 6 4 2

The text for this book is set in 14-point Perpetua.
Designed by Stephanie Bart-Horvath

Library of Congress Cataloging-in-Publication Data

Lasky, Kathryn.
Alice Rose & Sam / Kathryn Lasky.
p.   cm.
Summary: Alice Rose, an irrepressible twelve-year-old, shares adventures with
Mark Twain, an outlandish reporter on her father's newspaper in Virginia City,
Nevada, during the 1860s.
ISBN 0-7868-0336-3 (trade)—ISBN 0-7868-2277-5 (library)
1. Twain, Mark, 1835–1910—Juvenile fiction. [1. Twain Mark, 1835–1910—
Fiction. 2. Friendship—Fiction. 3. Virginia City (Nev)—Fiction.] I. Title.
PZ7.L3274Al 1997
[Fic]—dc21   97-40132

For Mary Ward

Chapter 1

ALICE ROSE TUCKER ground the toe of her boot into the gray gritty dirt. It was ugly. Downright ugly, this dirt. This ground. This earth! The thought struck her hard. One more thing to hate. One more item for her hate list. Not all the earth, but this earth right here, just outside of Virginia City—and, of course, in and all around Virginia City, Nevada. It didn't matter that deep in this earth veins of silver ran about willy-nilly. Nothing sparkled up where Alice Rose stood, and now, into this ugly earth they had just put the coffins of her mother and new baby sister.

The cemetery was a half mile outside of Virginia City, a town that was stuck in a gulch, hanging off the side of a mountain. Out here where the land was flat was the only place you could shove dead people without having them fall out of their coffins down the mountainside.

Alice Rose had this baby sister for all of two hours and seventeen minutes. And she had a mother for twelve years and four days. The four extra days were because her mother refused to die on her birthday. Suddenly two tears sprang up hot and stingy. She clamped her mouth shut tight. She hadn't really cried that much. She wasn't sure why. But the notion of her mother refusing to die on her birthday made her suspect that maybe, just maybe, her mother had found out about her hate list and didn't want Alice Rose to add her very own birthday to that list.

Well, she couldn't think about that now. She shifted her gaze to the second mound. It was barely a mound. Hardly looked like a grave, for that matter, more like a cake buried there in the gray dirt. How could she ever hate Nancy, even if her mother had died having her? She was tiny and perfect, and although she had lived for only two hours and seventeen minutes, she had opened her eyes and looked straight at Alice Rose. She seemed to know Alice Rose was her big sister. And her eyes were beautiful. They weren't that no color deep gray that babies are born with. They were a deep but clear blue. Like a periwinkle.

That's why, in Alice Rose's mind, Nancy was not really Nancy but Periwinkle, or Perry for short.

There were little Tucker babies planted all over the plains and prairies and deserts of the west. And Alice Rose had named them all for flowers. Near Carson City, Nevada, there was a Susan Daisy Tucker. In Central City, Colorado, there was an Eleanor Lily, and in Golden there was the only boy. She had named him Charles Columbine. She had dreamed of calling him C. C. Flowers were on Alice Rose's like list. And since she had always wanted a brother or sister, and since her middle name was Rose, she thought it made good sense to name a new baby sister or brother after a flower.

There was always so much commotion between the birthing and the dying that somehow her parents never got to the second name. But Alice Rose did. So across the frontier, her little ghost siblings bloomed like flowers with their secret flower names. Now there was no chance for more. She sighed a deep, weary sigh. Jewel Petty shot her a glance.

Jewel Petty was on Alice Rose's hate list. Jewel Petty wanted Alice Rose to cry, cry out loud, cry hard and let

herself be crushed to Jewel Petty's immense bosom and
get her cheek clawed by Jewel Petty's ugly brooch. The
brooch was on the hate list, too. Alice Rose turned her
head toward Jewel Petty and gave her the meanest look she
could muster, given that she was feeling as downright rotten as she was right now. You had to feel halfway decent to
give a really rank, mean as hell look. But she did all right.

Detta, who was standing near Jewel Petty, bit her lip
lightly. There wasn't much that surprised a hurdy-gurdy
girl, but this look from Alice Rose did. Alice Rose caught
the surprise. Tough. Detta wasn't on Alice Rose's hate list,
nor was she on her like list, so she couldn't spend too
much time worrying about Detta's reactions. Alice Rose
let her mind wander and ponder a spell on Detta. Boy oh
boy, did Detta look rotten. It was hard on hurdy-gurdy
girls being out this early in the morning, in the bright,
harsh sunlight. The carmine color painted on her lips was
smeary, and something blue was melting above her eyelids.
Her rouged cheeks were all streaky to boot. There were
rips in her parasol, and she was surely going to burn up her
shoulders. A hankie was stuffed in the neckline of her dress
to cover the fleshy little crack between her breasts. It was

very nice of Detta to do that, Alice Rose thought, because she knew that Detta's chest was her best feature. The rest of her had really gone to the dogs. She had deep lines and scrawny arms and her dyed hair looked like a hay bale caught fire. Detta had definitely seen better days. And that dress! The ruffles were in tatters and now covered with this ugly, gritty dirt. They looked like mashed-up animal guts, a dusty mauve. To top it off, her beauty spot—all the hurdy-gurdy girls pasted them on—had slipped over to her ear.

The minister's voice droned on. "To every thing there is a season and a time to every purpose under heaven. A time to be born, and a time to die; a time to plant, and a time to pluck up that which is planted; and a time to weep and a time to laugh; a time to mourn and a time to dance; a time to rend and a time to sew, a time to keep silence and a time to speak; a time to love and a time to hate."

The service was finally over. Alice Rose slipped her hand into her father's and they walked out through the small group of people, all dabbing their tears. "It was lovely, just lovely." Jewel Petty sniffed and poked at the corners of her eyes with a hankie.

"Lovely, lovely," Jewel's voice cawed. "Wasn't it lovely, dear?"

Now what could possibly be lovely about burying your mother and baby sister out in this godforsaken desert country? Lordy, she wished Eilley Orrum were here. Eilley Orrum would never say anything stupid like that. But Eilley was off on her Grand Tour.

"I do so love that passage from Ecclesiastes that the reverend read," Jewel continued. "A time to be born and a time to die." But, thought Alice Rose, poor little Periwinkle had to do it all in the space of two hours and seventeen minutes. "A time to weep." Jewel's eyes peered into Alice Rose's expectantly, but Alice Rose lanced her with another poisonous glance. There could be no doubt as to what time Alice Rose was thinking about. "Come on, Dad, it's time to go." She tugged at her father's hand, and Stan Tucker, heat-dazed and griefstricken, followed his only child down the path that led to the dirt road that twisted up to the town that was stuck in a gulch hanging off the side of a mountain.

Chapter 2

ALICE ROSE AND HER FATHER climbed the rickety, narrow stairs to their apartment in the Bigelow building on C Street. The minute they walked in, they were ambushed by the silence and the emptiness of the place. How odd, after months of complaining about how cramped the two rooms were, how decent life was virtually impossible, the space now seemed huge. The blistering sun slid through the windows and laid down two perfect rectangles of light on the wood floor. Dust motes spun in slow, lazy dances around them.

"We got any lemonade left, A. R.?" Her father called Alice Rose A. R. for short. She did not particularly like it, and in her mind it wasn't for short. It did not take any longer to say her full name, but it was short in terms of space—page space. Stan Tucker was a newspaperman, and newspapermen thought in terms of space. Columns were so many inches long, headlines ran so many columns wide, in type that was so many points big. A very small point size was agate, which was halfway between a pearl (five points) and a slug (six points). Alice Rose couldn't help but think that, in her father's mind, her name was just plain easier in agates. She knew she probably made too much of it, but her mother had always called her Alice Rose, never just Alice, never just Rose, and once in a while Alicia Rosa. Her mother had liked Italian things and was artistic. She had a book of Italian love poems and another one of pictures, beautiful black-and-white engravings of famous Roman ruins. When they would read the poems together or look at the pictures, Carrie Tucker would call her daughter Alicia Rosa. Alice Rose knew her father loved her probably as much as her mother. He just had a different way of showing it—agate type, no poetry.

"Yes, there's lemonade, but it'll be warm."

"That's okay. Long as it's wet."

Alice Rose went to the closet of a kitchen and opened the insulated tin box where they kept blocks of ice. They had kept it full of ice when her mother was sick and dying, but since she had died two days ago it didn't seem so important. They had only used the ice to cool her mother down from the fevers, never wasting a chip on a glass of water or lemonade.

She came back with two glasses filled. They sat down across from each other at the table. Suddenly the table seemed vast, nearly continental in its expanse. It was ridiculous, just the two of them sitting there. They looked up briefly at each other and blinked, each feeling a kind of embarrassment, as strangers might feel if they found themselves suddenly seated together.

"Well, well." Her father sighed and tapped his fingers on the table, then remembered to take a drink of the lemonade. Empty talk, empty gestures that seemed to echo the emptiness of the room. The words rumbled around like loose kegs on wooden planks.

"You know," Alice Rose began to speak, but somehow the two words got caught back in her throat and were strangled before becoming whole. "You know," she began again. Her voice was small and tight and parched. She didn't want these words thundering about, mocking them in this empty place. "I don't like it that she and Nancy are up there with all those murderers."

"What are you talking about, A. R.?"

"You know it's just a bunch of scum up there, Dad, in that cemetery."

"Well, they're not all murderers, Alice. Some of them have been murdered." She found this small consolation. "And they just buried that preacher fellow up there last week."

"Oh, Daddy, he wasn't any preacher. Dan De Quille said he saw him selling some snake oil remedy five years ago down in Carson City and he got into a pile of trouble with some preacher's daughter. That's how he probably learned to fake being a preacher. A fast learner. Just plain quick." She paused, then added, "But not quick enough. Johnny Gutt got him without half trying." Johnny Gutt was a gunslinger with a very bad temper, and he was very quick.

"Hrrum." Stan Tucker growled low and set his glass down with a solid tap on the table. He had heard the same about the fellow but he didn't know his daughter had. Came from hanging around the *Enterprise*'s office too much.

Alice Rose bit her lip deciding if she would say what was really on her mind. Finally she spoke. Suddenly the sounds weren't empty or meaningless. The words were real. "You think we ought to go back out there before dark and put a coyote cheat . . ." She never finished the sentence.

Her father's face darkened, but his voice was light. "Well, well, well." He began to stand up. Hadn't she known that this would be the way? When the talk got too real for Stan Tucker, when the dream of a claim petered out into a bunch of worthless tailings, he was out the door. Years ago, before Alice Rose was born, Stan Tucker had been bitten by the gold and silver bugs. He had given up a good job back East as editor in chief of a newspaper in Massachusetts to follow his dreams. His first dream had been to marry Alice Rose's mother. His second dream was to find precious metals. The second dream had bankrupted him, but he refused to give it up. He always had to be near a place where, if he had the time and the cash, he could pan or dig for gold or silver. So ever since Alice Rose could remember, they had lived in mining towns. As long as the towns were big enough to have a small newspaper, her father could make enough to put food on the table and a roof over their heads.

He patted her on the head. "Strawberry blonde," he commented inanely. Dirty blonde, she thought. "Now don't you go worrying about something like that. You know the undertaker did his finest. Lordy, I paid him a week's salary. He should. You think those murderers pay that well?"

A chill ran up Alice Rose's spine. If he just hadn't said the word *salary*. Why did he have to speak that way? He was burying his own wife, his infant daughter, her mother, her sister. Salary! He knew as well as she did that coyotes didn't care about salary. They always struck when the grave was fresh and it wasn't any secret that the best wood never went for coffins. No, the best wood went to reinforce the shafts in the chambers of the Ophir, the mine that was the very heart and soul of the mighty Comstock Lode. There was only one thing that could stop a coyote from tearing apart a fresh grave, and that was a boulder on top. They were called coyote cheats.

"I gotta get back to the office. I got to check the proofs for the next edition." He was halfway out the door. "I'll probably be late." That was all right with Alice Rose. She had plans. Plans to cheat a coyote.

Chapter 3

"DARN THAT MUTCH," she cursed under her breath as she tramped along the darkening road leading out of town to the cemetery. She had waited for that fool miner as long as she could. When he didn't show up she made a brief tour of the saloons and found him passed out in the alley behind the Glory Hole.

Mutch owed her one. Not one, she suddenly thought. He owed her two. Twice, she had filled out claim forms for him. He had traded her feet, feet in some spur off the main load that of course turned out to be no good. He'd been suckered in himself. Happened all the time. That was all people talked about in Virginia City—*feet*. Feet was probably the most spoken word in the town. People traded anything for feet in a vein that promised a big strike. Rich people would trade jewels; poor people, bread. Alice Rose hadn't given a hoot about feet. Mutch just didn't have anything else to trade when he asked her to fill out the claim form. He didn't know how to write, and half the time he was so drunk he couldn't think. She was just being nice when she filled out those forms. Well, nice got you nowhere, she thought as she tromped along the road. From now on it would be strictly cash.

She had no idea how she would move that rock alone. At that moment, she heard the first howl of a coyote. She quickened her pace.

The tombstones stood like stunted children against the purple sky. The moon rolled onto the horizon. Alice Rose thought she had remembered some good-sized rocks nearby where her mother and Periwinkle lay buried. If she could just move them. She'd brought a shovel, part of her father's large arsenal of gold-digging equipment.

In the deepening darkness, distances were deceiving and she came upon the graves all of a sudden. The thought flashed through her mind that something was different about Perry's. It had been a perfect little cake before. In one instant, the top of the grave erupted. A scalding hiss peeled through the darkness. The most enormous rattler she had ever seen coiled and reared its head. She gasped. It was as if her breath had been sucked right out of her. The head of the snake was weaving, the tongue flicking in and out. It was striking again and again, striking in some primeval fury at the rising moon. Then it swung its head toward Alice Rose and fixed her in its slitted eyes. The head seemed to swell. It hissed even more furiously, as if daring Alice Rose to pass another step closer to Nancy Periwinkle's grave. Suddenly it seemed as if the entire world had shrunk up and there was only this small sphere filled with herself, the snake, and the graves of her mother and sister.

"How dare you!" she flung out the words. "How dare you!" she screamed. No damned snake would sit on her baby sister's grave. She lunged toward the rattler, her shovel raised. Never had she seen, felt, and reacted with such clarity. It was as if she had locked that weaving head in the thin crosshairs of a scope right in her brain. The shovel sliced through the air. There was a tiny *snick* and the head flew through the night, its tongue still flicking against the darkening sky. Then there was this odd pocket of silence in which the only sound was the last rattling of the snake's still twitching body.

Alice Rose had heard that you were supposed to bury rattlesnake heads, but it seemed downright unchristian to bury one in a cemetery, even it was filled mostly with murderers and their victims. And she certainly didn't want this snake anywhere near her mother and Periwinkle. So she scooped up the mutilated remains and took them to the far side of the cemetery where the land fell away into a deep canyon, and she threw the whole nasty thing over the edge. Then she got down to the business at hand—moving rocks.

At first it went quickly. She found several heavy but round and rollable rocks. Enough to cover Perry's grave. But they ran out, and her mother's grave was just half covered. There was a big rock not fifteen feet away that would have done the job, but the thought of moving it was unimaginable. She didn't know what else to do but give it a try.

After ten minutes, she managed to get the shovel under one edge and standing on the handle, using it as a

fulcrum, she could just about budge it. It would take
more than budging, however. The night was now laced
with the howls of coyotes, but the thought of going to
look for better, more rollable rocks was not appealing.
What if she found more rattlesnakes instead? The slope
above the cemetery was washed in moonlight. She was
standing on the shovel handle bouncing slightly in hopes
of dislodging the rock a bit more when the breeze that
riffled her hair suddenly brought a funny little tune down
the slope. She stopped her bouncing. It was whistling.
Someone was whistling in the night out here! Wasn't that
just the limit! Then, an immense shadow slid across the
moon-washed slope. Alice Rose could not make out the
shape. It looked like a person, but there seemed to be a
tail streaming from the head! The whistling stopped suddenly. So did the shadow. Alice Rose blinked. She realized
that she, too, cast a long shadow that slid into this one.
And now the figure that cast the first shadow seemed to
be trying to figure out the shape of her shadow.

"Ay yah!" came the call, and then she heard a scuttling
sound. Within a matter of seconds a man was standing
before her. He was not much taller than Alice Rose and

he wore a Chinaman's small, boxlike hat. The shadow tail that had streamed out in the moonlight was his pigtail. Virginia City was full of Chinese people, and all of the men wore a similar costume. "Miss, what you doing here all by yourself? Not safe place for nice young lady." Then he paused and looked down. He muttered something in Chinese. " 'Splain what you try to do here standing on stick."

But before she could explain he said. "Ah! You try to move rock. Cheat coyote!" Then he brought his head closer. His dark tilted eyes were soft and questioning. "You bury Daddy? Mummy? You want to protect?"

"Mummy," Alice Rose whispered. "And ba—" But the word just blubbered out, and for the first time since her mother and sister had died, Alice Rose really wept. She had wept inside tears for days, but now they spilled out in a torrent. The Chinaman drew out a large silk handkerchief.

As soon as she had dried her tears he announced, "No more worry. I help you move rock. We cheat those coyotes. I move rock all the time."

"You do?"

"Sure. I work for Union Pacific Railroad. I lay tracks. Move rocks all time."

"Yeah, but I don't have any dynamite."

"No, no. Other ways. Other tools." He paused. "My name Hop Sing. What your name, little girl? I come now from Carson City." He nodded toward the south in the direction of Carson City, which was twenty or more miles beyond the ridge over which he had appeared.

"Alice Rose. Alice Rose Tucker. Virginia City."

"All right, Alice Rose Tucker. I be right back. I left my mule back up slope."

Alice Rose would never figure out exactly how Hop Sing, who was only an inch or so taller than she was, ever moved that rock. She had seen magicians come through town and been less impressed. But if any human being could see through a job, could, in this case, see through a rock, gauge its points of least resistance, then calculate where gravity might give him assistance and where mechanical advantage could be applied to the maximum, it was Hop Sing. With a crowbar, a shovel, ropes, and a hand crank winch, all carried aboard the most pathetic excuse for a mule Alice Rose had ever seen, Hop Sing moved the rock within half an hour.

They walked back into Virginia City together. And as the moon rose higher, their two shadows overlapped on the road. At the corner of C Street and Taylor they stopped.

"You go down there then turn left onto D Street. Then go down to the next street below, E Street. That's where Chinatown is and you'll find your friend, Hop Sing," Alice Rose said. Just at that moment a barrel-shaped man reeled out from the swinging doors of the Sazerac Saloon.

"Why, Alice Rose!" he warbled in a high voice.

"Mr. Daggett! Get hold of yourself!"

The man clasped his arms around himself, held tight, and giggled madly. "I don't know how he gets out a column of copy but he does, several every week. The man's a walking whiskey barrel," she muttered to Hop Sing.

"Now, I'm not drunk, Miss Alice. I'm steady as can be." He looked up. "It's the moon that's drunk up there!" He laughed at this as if it were just about the funniest thing in the world, then staggered down the street. Alice Rose supposed her father was in there—not quite drunk, he never was—with Dan De Quille and Steve Gillis from the *Enterprise*.

"Well, good night, Alice Rose Tucker," Hop Sing said, and shook her hand.

"Good night, Hop Sing, and thank you."

The mule made an impolite noise. Alice Rose turned up C Street to go home. She slept well knowing that under hundreds, maybe thousands of pounds of rock, her mother and little Periwinkle were safe. She sure had cheated those coyotes—with the help of Hop Sing, who'd been worth fourteen Mutches gilt in gold.

Chapter 4

"HOMEMADE SIN dipped in misery!" Alice Rose spoke solemnly and pressed her lips together. Detta looked at herself in the mirror. The dress hung off her like sails that had lost their wind, the ruffles faded and dusty. "You deserve better. I can make you something really pretty. Mr. Rachman just got in some real stiff taffeta. It'll stand up in a tornado. It's so slick the dust will skid right off it. All sorts of colors—peacock blue, emerald green. You'd look really fine in emerald green, Detta. Perfect for your eyes." Detta cocked her head and opened her eyes a little wider as she studied her reflection.

"How much will it cost me, Alice Rose? You know I ain't making as much as I used to. Not since that new gal

Ella showed up. All the hurdy-gurdy girls' business is off. You know that Ella, she's pulling in five dollars a dance. And the other night a fella gave her twenty!" A hurdy-gurdy girl normally got twenty-five cents a dance and sometimes a tip of a dollar, but five dollars was rare. And twenty, unheard of!

"Twenty!" gasped Alice Rose. "Well, I'll tell you what, Detta. I'll make you the prettiest dress in Virginia City and I'll just charge you for the cost of materials for this first one. But then you got to do my advertising for me and don't you dare tell the other girls I didn't charge you."

"Why, Alice Rose, you're a peach!" Detta's thin face broke into a smile. "And you know what?"

"What?"

"If any fool miner tips me twenty dollars I'm giving you ten percent."

Alice Rose smiled brightly, even though she thought that there was about as much chance of a man tipping Detta twenty dollars as those feet that Mutch had traded her actually paying off. But one never knew. Silver dust did funny things to men's minds. A fellow comes in right after a strike and all of a sudden Detta looks not just good in her new dress, but beautiful. And the fellow starts pouring money all over her.

Alice Rose's mother had been an excellent seamstress and had brought in a portion of the family income through her sewing and fine tailoring. Mostly, she had made serviceable, no-nonsense clothing: dusters, those ubiquitous long flaring coats worn by both men and women to fend off dust storms, mud, and rain. She also made serge trousers, frock coats, and the occasional Sunday go-to-church dress for prosperous ladies. Alice Rose had learned a lot about sewing from her mother. She knew how to overlock seams for durability, how to fashion a welt pocket, how to do a "flat nip," an invention of her mother's that was halfway between a tuck and a pleat. She knew how to set a sleeve to perfection, she knew gores and darts. But the idea of becoming a dressmaker for the hurdy-gurdy girls had never occurred to Alice Rose until the day after she had returned from the cemetery.

A letter had arrived that day from her aunt Eugenia in Boston. She savored Aunt Eugenia's letters and liked to read them when she was alone. The letter had been addressed to her mother. Poor Aunt Eugenia didn't know yet that her sister was dead.

The first part was hard to get through for it was filled with assurances that this time her dear sister Carrie would have a healthy baby. Then Aunt Eugenia had launched into Boston news and her activities. She had met with her poetry society and attended several lectures at the Lyceum. Her four lively daughters had been to two ice-cream socials in one month and the older girls had attended a cotillion dance, but generally such festivities were not so numerous because of the war. Aunt Eugenia wrote: "It is my feeling that there is an overly frivolous social schedule during this terrible war, even if much of it revolves around bandage rolling or raising funds for war widows."

Aunt Eugenia was not a frivolous person. She deplored unseemly displays in costume, manners, or food. She would have hated Virginia City. Her mother had a daguerreotype that showed Eugenia to be a plain woman with a pince-nez perched on her beaklike nose, her hair skinned back to reveal a high bony forehead with a sharp widow's peak.

"I know that my girls love putting on their party dresses," Aunt Eugenia wrote, "and Lily just had a lovely azure one made with inverted gores, but I do worry. For how in truth does dancing a quadrille advance the art of mental refinement?"

Truth. Dancing. Inverted gores. The words had burst upon Alice Rose's brain like stars in a heavenly transit and then, all of a sudden, a constellation formed in her imagination. How often had she longed to go to Boston, to live with her four girl cousins and attend the Boston seminary. The *truth* was she needed money to go to Boston. And money could be got by sewing. She looked over at the cupboard. Its doors were open and inside was a stack of fabrics—all tough fabrics in dull colors—worsteds, serge, boiled wool, tweeds, and even canvas. These were the sensible fabrics her mother dealt with. They hardly ever wore out. But satins, cottons, and taffetas worn to hell and back by the hurdy-gurdy girls sure did!

Who, after all, was really dependable in this fool town? Who would never try to trade you a foot of some no-good claim rather than give you money? Who never got drunk (except of course for Buffalo Jo, but she hardly counted)?

Why, the hurdy-gurdy girls! They were always sober. They paid in cash, and a lot of them, Detta, for instance, were starting to look like something the cat dragged in from the mud and dust of this hellhole of a desert town.

Alice Rose's course was clear. She must become fashion consultant, dress designer, and seamstress to this unholy lot of bedraggled women. Detta would be her first customer. If she could make a truly spectacular dress for Detta, the other girls might follow.

"Trust me, Detta, emerald green's your color. Now how 'bout it?"

"It's a deal, Alice Rose."

camp stool in her bloomers. Dang it if the stuff isn't still being hauled up there by the barrel load."

"Don't swear, Simon, and I wish you'd find your specs. This is going very slow with you squint-reading."

"Well, Priscilla, if you wrote proper instead of these chicken tracks . . ."

"Here, I'll read the rest," Alice Rose offered. "Forty-five hook-and-eyes, five yards plain black rickrack trim."

"Rickrack trim?" said Mrs. Rachman, scurrying down the ladder toward the notions cabinet. "That seems mighty ordinary, don't you think, Alice Rose? I mean for Miss Eilley."

"I wouldn't know." Alice Rose sighed. "You never can tell with Miss Eilley."

"Isn't that the truth. Anything else on that list, Alice?"

"Nope, that's it. I can deliver this for you if you want."

"Oh, that's mighty kind of you, sweetheart. Now what can we do for you?" Priscilla leaned over the counter and patted her hand. "How's your dad?"

"Fine," Alice Rose mumbled. The worst thing about having someone die was the sympathy. She knew they all meant well, but for some reason, all these tender expres-

Chapter 5

"She needs fifteen yards of buckram. Heaviest weight." Mr. Rachman squinted at the piece of paper as his small wife scrambled up a ladder toward a bolt of material.

"Fifteen yards, Simon? What's she going to do with fifteen yards? This stuff is like iron. A little bit to reinforce a bodice is all that is ever needed."

"Maybe not if the bodice is like Miss Eilley's and going to have to support the crown jewels."

Alice Rose had just walked through the doors of Rachman's dry goods store. "Miss Eilley is back? Since when?"

"She most certainly is, since last night. And she brough half the loot from every palace and kingdom in Europe imagine the queen of England's been left sitting o sions made her feel like someone's slightly injured pet. "I came in for some of that new taffeta. I need about nine yards of the emerald green and . . ." She paused. What if she faced the ruffles with the peacock blue? Wouldn't that be something! "And maybe about five of the peacock blue."

Priscilla got down the bolts and measured the fabric. Alice Rose counted out the money that Detta had advanced her. After dropping off the material at her apartment, Alice Rose headed out C Street. She soon picked up a ride on a buckboard going her way, for it was a far piece, over ten miles, to where Eilley Orrum's palace sprawled across the brown hills above Lake Washoe.

Alice Rose followed a grand piano and half a dozen spindly little gold chairs into the front hall of Eilley Orrum's and her husband, Sandy Bower's, mansion. Eilley swept down the immense staircase and embraced Alice Rose. "Sorry kiddo, about your mother. A good, honest, and smart lady." Alice Rose sighed with near plea-sure. She no longer felt like someone's gimpy pet.

Five minutes later she was down on her hands and knees in Eilley's second-floor parlor studying a detailed illustration of a dress design. "It's kind of like a gusset, Alice Rose, but it ain't. Musheur Gagelin calls it a 'godet.' We just didn't have time to wait around for him to make me another dress in Paris, but I told him about your mother, who could give any one of his seamstresses a run for their money. Didn't know of course what would happen to her. But I figure you're every bit as smart." Something glowed warm and bright inside Alice Rose. Eilley continued, "You can't be around a smart lady like your mother and not pick up something. I've seen the way you two were together. Remember that Christmas dress she made me two years ago? You sat there so quiet and still just watching your mother's fingers while she fitted me. It takes a certain amount of intelligence, if you ask me, to be able to sit still, watch, and learn. Not many people around here have that kind of smarts. Mostly they are just mouthing off all the time. But you do. So what do you think, Alice? Be an honor to me, and I think to your mother, if you'd do this."

Alice Rose felt a jumble of wonderful feelings inside her. She *did* remember her mother's quick fingers and the way she squinted when she backed off from the dress during a fitting to see how it fell.

She wrinkled her brow. "I think I can do it, but we can't use that flimsy stuff that's in the rest of the skirt."

"What about the buckram you brought me?"

"Naw, that's too heavy. I'm sure you got something over there that'll work." Alice Rose nodded toward the tall stack of fabrics against the wall.

"I knew you could do it, gal!" Eilley clapped her on the back. "Now let's go outside and set a piece on my porch and I'll tell you about my Grand Tour."

They had just settled down with tall glasses of lemonade, and Eilley was going on about how in the elegant European palaces nobody ever called a porch a porch. "Pergolas, porticos, pavilions—very popular that one, p—" Another *P* word for porch had started to form Eilley's lips, when she jumped up so suddenly that her fancy new wig went slightly askew. "Well, I'll be!" she cried in delight, and raced over to the edge of the porch. She peered down into the bare dirt. "Lookee there. It's a good sign, Alice Rose! A mighty good sign!"

Alice Rose followed her to the edge of the porch and looked down. "All I see is one of those big old desert snails."

Eilley jerked herself up, her small black eyes sparkled. Even at her full height she was still a shade shorter than Alice Rose. "Alice Rose, you mean to tell me that you don't know the importance of a snail? How a snail signifies?"

"No, ma'am, I can't say as I do."

Eilley sighed deeply and looked down in a gesture of despair. The accretion of chins beneath her plump face receded into her neck as she bowed her head in thought and clamped her mouth shut. "Okay, dear." She took Alice Rose's hand. "Let me tell you a thing or two about snails and my life and how I would give a bucket of tarot cards, a bushel of tea leaves, and all the fortune tellers from here to Sacramento for one snail, any snail. They don't have to be special."

"What about your peepstone?" Alice Rose asked.

"Peepstones and snails aren't exactly the same thing. Peepstones tell the future. Snails they just, well, hint at it. You have to be smarter to read a snail's track than to look in a peepstone. Looking in a peepstone is like shooting fish in a barrel next to reading snail tracks. I built this whole mansion just from looking in my peepstone and watching the pictures. It was why I never needed an architect."

Alice Rose looked up at the balconies, the elaborate stone walls, the porticos, and inside there was the marble, the painted ceilings, the silver doorknobs. It was hard to imagine that a snail could outdo such a peepstone.

"I was a wee girl back in Scotland . . ." Whenever Eilley started talking about Scotland, where she had been born, a slight burr crept into her voice. Her black eyes softened as if lost in the mist of a Scottish morning long, long ago. "It was May Day and—" She broke away for a minute. "I haven't told you this story about what Scottish lassies do on May Day?"

"No, ma'am." Alice Rose shook her head.

Eilley continued, "Well, it was May Day and what young girls do is take their writing slates out onto the moor at dawn. Mind you, that is the best time, that's when you can find the most snails and when you can get the most accurate reading. It's when the snail's brain is the clearest."

Snail's brain! Alice Rose blinked. She had never thought about snails having brains. Eilley continued,

"Well, I found me a snail, put down my slate right smack-dab in its path, and sure enough that snail heads right for it—lickety-split! Well, not exactly lickety-split. I'm getting carried away with my story here." She did not, however, take back her reference to the snail's brain. "The snail sort of chugged up there and started going across my slate, leaving its silvery twisty trail. Well, I got down on my hands and knees. I was about fifteen you know."

"Fifteen? I thought you said you were a wee girl."

"Well, I was. Fifteen is wee when you're lookin' down on it from the mountaintop of fifty!"

"Oh," said Alice Rose.

Eilley resumed her story. "We all, as girls of that age do, had marriage on our minds." Alice Rose wondered if in three years she would have marriage on her mind. She doubted it. "And getting out of this tattered little Highland village, of course. So we would study the curly track of a snail, for it was said that if you looked hard enough you could see the letters of someone who would become very important in your life. Who would change your life forever."

"So it wouldn't have to be a husband?"

"No, not at all. It could be any old person who would change the track of your life. So I looked down and at first I saw two letters—*E* and *H*—plain as anything, or so I thought. But then, as the sun rose and the light struck those letters at a new angle I thought maybe they didn't look so much like an *E* and an *H*, but maybe more like *S* and *B*." Alice Rose couldn't figure out how Eilley could get those letters mixed up. "Well, in any case, I decided to go with my first reading." She paused. "Big mistake." Eilley let the words sink in. "Edward Hunter, a traveling Mormon preacher, came through the very next week, and by golly if I didn't up and marry him and come to America. He was a bishop in the church and it wasn't long before I found out that all while he was sweet-talking through his whiskers to me, that the three nieces who had just arrived weren't no nieces at all but wives one, two, and three!"

"Everyone knows Mormons have more than one wife, Eilley," Alice Rose said.

"Not me. I was a wee mite of a thing from Scotland. Maybe down in the lowlands they do such mongrelish things, but not in the Highlands I tell you! What did I know about wives by the dozen—polygamy they call it. Fancy word for a lowdown, nasty business."

"What did you do?"

Eilley's face turned stony. Her small black eyes narrowed and her littlest chin, the one that sat on top of the others, dimpled as she set her jaw. The small mouth in the middle snapped out the words. "I was so dang mad I went out to the barn and strangled his prize rooster—another polygamist if there ever was one, only difference was the feathers." She exhaled a small jet of air through her nostrils. "Then I went and bought me a divorce—fifteen dollars. Best money I ever spent."

"Then what happened?"

"Went to work selling calico and stuff in Reese's general store in Salt Lake City. Wouldn't go to none of their Saturday night dances down there. Just hunting ground for these fellows to line up wives eighteen, nineteen, and twenty."

"So you should have read *S, B* instead of *E, H?*"

"I certainly should have, but it took a little more time to figure it out. Man came into the general store one day. He had no money just some trading material. Awful-looking old stuff—battered cup and a smelly blanket, but wrapped up in that smelly blanket was a big, smoky-looking glass ball."

"Your peepstone!" Alice Rose exclaimed.

"You bet your butt!" laughed Eilley. "I knew it was special right off the bat. I cleaned it up and I had a piece of black velvet that I had snitched from that fool, my former husband's church. I set the ball down on it. Right about sunset it was, and the rays of the sun, all orange and red, swirled like blood in an egg yolk." Eilley's voice grew soft now. "I saw a mountaintop, then I saw a valley and a lake—blue like this one." She nodded toward Washoe. "Not like that smelly piss pot of white salt down there in Salt Lake City. And I knew where I had to go."

Alice Rose knew the rest of the story. It was famous. How Eilley had come up to the Nevada territory and built herself a cabin in Gold Canyon, a mile south of Virginia City, before there even was a Virginia City. But the boom was just starting and there were miners galore. Eilley ran a boardinghouse for miners, cooking and doing their laundry and offering them a bed—never hers! She kept peering into her peepstone and she knew that it was in Nevada that sooner or later she would make her fortune. One miner, Lemuel Sanford Bowers, offered her ten feet of his fifty-foot claim in exchange for room and board. He was a nice fellow, and although she rarely traded room and board for feet, she had a feeling about this man. "And when I found out that everyone called him Sandy for short," Eilley said, "I remembered the snail's track, and up and married him the next day. But of course, I had one rule." She lifted her finger. "And you know that one." Alice Rose nodded. It was the no-sell rule. The peepstone had told her not to sell. People had been selling like crazy that summer of 1859. Together, Sandy and Eilley had a combined twenty feet. "A man offered us $400,000 that summer. Sandy was tempted, but the peepstone said no. So, here we sit." Eilley leaned back in her chair and surveyed her domain. "You know that solid silver tea service I had made to give to the queen of England."

"Yep. Did you get to meet her?"

"No!"

"Why not?"

"Would you believe that the queen will not receive divorced people?"

"Receive them? You just wanted to meet her."

"That's what they call it, 'receive.' "

"Oh, Eilley!" Alice Rose sighed.

"Don't 'Oh, Eilley' me. I don't give a twit for queens like that. Besides, Sandy ordered me a nice little throne."

"A nice little throne?" Alice Rose asked. Well, some did call Eilley the Silver Queen of the Comstock.

"Yes. It'll be coming soon. Finest cabinetmaker in all of Scotland making it. I'm going to sit on it, and I'll receive anybody as long as they're nice folks and make me laugh—even Mormons!"

Alice Rose grew silent and thought not about queens and thrones and silver but Eilley's words about getting out when she had been a wee thing of fifteen. "Eilley," Alice Rose said suddenly. "If I'd run down there to where that snail is and studied his track and saw some letters, would they tell me about who might change my life?"

"Oh, Lord, no child. You have to go and find your own snail. I spotted that one. And what did I tell you about snail's brains and finding them in the mornings."

"Oh, yes." Alice Rose remembered now, although it

seemed to her that snail's brains were a fairly easy thing to forget.

Alice Rose got tired of looking for snails all the way back into town. She supposed she would have to come much earlier in the morning, but the notion that she would find one creeping along the main street in or out of town didn't seem likely. With all the wagon and foot traffic, there was a good chance that any snail would be smashed flatter than a flapjack. No, she would have to go elsewhere. She supposed she could go to the kitchen of the International Hotel. She had heard a rumor that they served snails—and even oysters and cow's brains—in the dining room. They were considered fancy French delicacies. She loved to visit the hotel, but she had no desire ever to eat there. That was not her idea of good food. But thinking about the hotel did give her an idea as she was coming into town. There was something else that it had and she loved. An elevator!

She took a slight detour, walking down C Street until she came to the corner of Union and C where the International Hotel stood, the finest hotel west of the

Mississippi, and the only hotel with an elevator east of San Francisco and west of Chicago. Riding the elevator was one of Alice Rose's favorite pastimes. But it was difficult if grouchy old Spittin' McCrae was on duty. Spittin' McCrae had been a millionaire for all of four days. But then his claim turned out to be no good, like many of the original Comstock claims. Such claims were often staked for possession of the surface ground in the tradition of placer mining. But once the surface ore was removed, there was still the richest lode in the veins. To follow the geological dips and spurs and angles of a vein led to much legal wrangling. This was how Spittin' McCrae lost his. The legal disputes made rich a lot of lawyers who now dined on caviar and oysters and champagne at the International Hotel.

McCrae was finally reduced to serving the very men who had fleeced him through their lawyer fees. He had, however, thought up a strange method of revenge: spitting in their food before he was to serve them. Word got out, but he threatened to do worse if they fired him from the hotel. So they put him on elevator duty. He did his job in a harmless manner, except for boring hotel guests with his endless stories of being fleeced by lawyers. And he did not look kindly on Alice Rose's frequent demands for rides. Alice Rose didn't mind. She could put up with a lot for the marvelous smooth sensation the elevator provided. It was like floating up on a cloud of goose down. And of course, it could be very interesting if there was a load of passengers. Only the very best people stayed at the International. You could pick up a lot of information, and now that she thought about it, she might even get some fashion ideas for her new business. The Lord only knew how she was going to work that bit with Eilley's dress—that crazy gusset. Maybe there'd be a grand lady in the elevator who was wearing a dress with those things. Research! That was what she would tell Spittin' McCrae she was doing in his elevator.

Alice Rose made her way through the lobby of the hotel. It was a grand place with twisted gold gilt columns, palm trees in ornate tubs, and gentlemen in stiff frock coats carrying gold-topped canes and escorting ladies decked out in radiant splendor. The women's elaborate hairdos erupted with the feathers of the most exotic birds. Their white skin blazed with jewels. They made the hurdy-gurdy girls in the saloons look like chicken pickings. Alice Rose scanned the hems of several hoop skirts to see if they flared out with the special gussets, the godets. She made her way over to the elevator and was watching the hand on the dial above its door, indicating at which floor the elevator had stopped. There was a jangle of chains and a creak as it arrived. Maybe, just maybe, there would be a lady with godets behind the door when it slid open. Research, she would remember to tell Spittin' McCrae. That was her mission. She was just about to explain her new mission to Spittin' McCrae when the door opened.

"Alice Rose!"

She blinked in disbelief. "Hop Sing, what in heaven's name are you doing here?"

"I run elevator now."

"What happened to Spittin' McCrae? Did he spit on a passenger?"

"Worse."

"Worse?" Alice Rose's eyes widened. "You have to tell me, Hop Sing."

"Not ladylike talk, Alice Rose."

"Come on. I'm not a lady yet. I'm just a girl."

Hop Sing began to chuckle. "Like you know when dog go to make water on a tree."

"Oh, my word!" Alice Rose clapped her hands over her mouth.

"Yes. But all cleaned up now, you step in. Where you go?"

"Oh, anywhere. I'm not particular. I'm just here for the ride. Up, down—guess you can't go sideways in this thing."

For the next half hour, Alice Rose rode up and down with Hop Sing. She described her research project, the hunt for godets. Hop Sing said if he saw any lady wearing such a dress he would come and tell her. As she left the elevator Alice Rose said, "You know where I live now, and if I'm not there I might be over at the *Territorial Enterprise* office, or sometimes I go to the dump. The dump's a great place. You ought to come with me sometime. You can find anything in the dump. Maybe even a godet—who knows."

Chapter 6

HOTTER THAN HINGES . . . Hotter than the hubs of hell . . . Hot enough to scorch a grizzly's butt. It was simply too hot to sew, but she had nevertheless made good progress on Detta's dress. However, she still had no ideas for Eilley's irksome godet. It was September, the heat was still fierce, and the air in the apartment felt stiff as a board and still as death. Alice Rose could barely move herself. So she sat making up 'hot as' phrases. She wrote them down in her notebook. It was a reporter's notebook. Her father brought them to her from the office. She had already filled one and she was halfway through this one. She kept her hate list and her like list in it, as well as any random thoughts she might have about life.

"Hot enough to fry an egg on a bald man's head!" She looked at the words and suddenly an idea, a brilliant idea, exploded in her brain. She bet they were short on stories over at the *Territorial*. She'd bring those fellows a bucket of fresh lemonade and the best story idea yet.

"You are a sight for sore eyes, Miss Alice Rose." Rollin Daggett sighed as she entered the *Territorial Enterprise* offices at 27 North C Street.

"You look much improved yourself from the other evening Mr. Daggett," Alice Rose replied.

"You tell him, Alice!" bellowed Joe Goodman, the editor of the *Enterprise*.

Dan De Quille was fast asleep under his visored cap.

"How you doing, A. R.?" her father called. He and Steve Gillis, the compositor who laid up the type trays for printing, were leaning over looking into the innards of the steam press.

"How you doing, Dad? Brought you all some lemonade."

Stanley Tucker drew himself out of the shadows of the press. "Why, A. R., that's right nice of you. Thank you, sweetheart." Alice Rose felt a little pinch inside her. This was the first time her father had looked at her, really looked at her, in days. "Did you hear about Doc Willis's strike?"

"No," she replied slowly. Doctor Willis had tended her mother while she was sick and had delivered little Perry. They had been rather irritated with him at the time of the delivery, feeling that he had left too soon. Hadn't even stayed around for the two hours and seventeen minutes that Perry had lived, when he had clearly seen that the baby was in trouble and that there might be trouble coming for her mother.

"Well, I'll tell you sweetheart, he's hit it big. We're giving—how many inches is it, Joe—to the story?"

"Five—least five, Stan."

"Five inches. And quarter banner headline in fourteen-point type with three subheads in full agate."

Alice Rose felt a queasiness well up from somewhere deep in her gut. He was still just as silver crazy as ever. More so now since her mother had died. No one to hold him back, keep him steady. And the worst of it was that he had been equally mad at Dr. Willis, but now was it all okay, just because Doc Willis had struck it rich?

"Look, can anybody wake up Dan? I got a good idea for

a quaint." Quaints were the little stories that were Dan De Quille's specialty. They had absolutely no bearing on the truth whatsoever, but Dan De Quille was a fancier of science fiction and loved spinning his own inimitable brand of it in the pages of the *Territorial Enterprise*. They were Alice Rose's favorite part of the paper.

"Did I hear my name mentioned?" a voice drawled from under the visored cap. Two boots uncrossed themselves very slowly from the desktop where they were perched.

"Yes. Yours, Dan." Alice Rose spoke up. "I got the beatingest idea for a quaint."

"All right, Rosie. Let's hear it."

Alice Rose stuck her hand in her pocket and came up with an egg. She held it so all could see. "Yes?" said Dan.

"I was sitting back in our apartment thinking about how hot it is—hot as hinges—hot as the hubs of hell— hot enough to scorch a grizzly's butt—"

"Hot as election day in a hornet's nest," offered Rollin Daggett.

"Hotter than a burnt boot."

Alice Rose would let the boys play with this for a while

before she let loose with her final to-end-all-hot-as phrases. "Hot enough to wither a fence post," said Mac McCarthy in his broad Australian accent. There was a pause after McCarthy spoke.

"Ready fellows?" Alice Rose asked, lifting her egg into full view. All the newsmen's eyes were on her. "Hot enough to fry an egg on a bald man's head!" She then turned, smiled, and looked slowly at Rollin Daggett, who had a very large bald spot, and then to her father who had only a thin fringe of brown hair encircling his shiny skull.

"Genius!" Dan De Quille leaped up from his desk. "She's a prodigy. Stan, I hope you realize this. Okay, who's it going to be? Rollin or Stan? Who will offer up their marvelous dome for this entirely scientific experiment to be performed by none other than Herr Doktor Dan De Quille. Come on Rollin, do it! Do it!"

"No, I think, editorially speaking," Joe Goodman said, "that Stan has a little more territory to work with there. It'd be like branding calves in a tight pen to crack an egg on Rollin's head."

"How can I thank you?" Daggett replied quietly, and returned to his reading matter.

"What do I get for this?" Alice Rose's father suddenly asked.

"Well, as you know, Stan, I got no feet to trade," Joe Goodman said, "but it would make a right fine story. How about a champagne dinner at the International Hotel? Alice Rose included of course, since the whole thing is her idea."

"Wait a minute! Wait just a cotton-picking minute!" Rollin Daggett was rising from his chair. Wouldn't you know it, thought Alice Rose, as soon as liquor was mentioned Rollin Daggett got interested. But she was pleased her father had taken the bait. She could hardly believe that her father, who was never as jokey as the rest of the boys, would agree to having an egg cracked over his head.

"Nope, Daggett," her father was saying, "you're out of this. Besides it was A. R.'s idea. So it should be her dad who gets to do it."

"You don't mind, Dad, you really don't mind?"

"No, sweetheart. It's a dandy idea. Besides, I owe you a decent meal after all your hard work." Stan Tucker smiled at his daughter, a slow, soft smile. He didn't say "after all your hard work taking care of your mother," but she knew that was what he meant.

This was the problem, Alice Rose thought. She just never knew where her father was coming from. Sometimes he seemed so full of love and wanting to do the right thing for her and then other times he seemed so far away. It was as if she had to remind him that he was a father and had been a husband. She supposed that she never really doubted his love, but she sure did doubt his ability to concentrate on the people he was supposed to love and take care of.

Suddenly there was a bellow and a clatter. Something was thumping up the stairs. Another bump, a groan, and a rank odor seeped into the room. The men of the *Territorial Enterprise* and Alice Rose fell silent. Their heads turned expectantly to the door when a man stumbled in. He was covered from head to toe in alkali dust. His waist-length beard showed signs of being fiery red under the dust, and there were bits of hay tangled in the long matted strands. Alice Rose and the men stood speechless as the large man wavered before them. Joe Goodman took a step forward. "Josh? Sam Clemens?" he asked.

"Yes." said the man, and held out his hand. "My starboard leg seems unshipped. I'd like about one hundred yards of line. I think I'm falling to pieces." With that, he keeled over.

"Josh . . . it's Josh!" the men started to whisper.

"Josh?" repeated Alice Rose. "*That* Josh?"

"That's the one. The very one, A. R.," said her dad.

Everyone had been talking about Josh since he had started sending in his crazy letters some months before. The letters were hilarious, outlandish. Josh especially enjoyed poking fun at politicians.

Joe Goodman was now squatting by the crumpled man known as Josh. He groaned. "And this is the guy I looked high and low to hire," Joe Goodman said in dismay.

Josh stirred. "My good opinion of your paper began to decline rapidly when you began printing my letters; now that you've actually offered me a job, it's hit rock bottom."

Alice Rose giggled and the other men began to chuckle.

Josh hoisted himself to his feet. "But necessity is the mother of taking chances. So here I am reporting for duty."

Ophira, the office cat, had sidled up to Sam Clemens's

leg and seemed not offended by his odor. "Where, might I ask, have you arrived from, Mr. Clemens?"

"Sam, just Sam. Aurora."

"But there's no stage due in today from Aurora."

"I know. I walked."

"You *what?*" several men said at once. Alice Rose just stared with her mouth hanging open. Aurora was at least 130 miles away.

"I think a bath might be in order, Sam," Joe Goodman said. "Follow me. There's a tub downstairs in the backyard." Alice Rose watched as the strange man named Sam Clemens followed Goodman out and down the backstairs.

"Well, I never." Steve Gillis scratched his chin.

"Once he cleans up he'll fit right in," Dennis McCarthy said. Alice Rose had no doubt about that as she looked around at the journalists in the room. They were nothing more than a pack of overgrown boys, her father included. Sam Clemens was just like them. She could tell instantly. Yes, he would fit right in. She wondered, however, where in this world would she ever fit in. What would Aunt Eugenia say if she had been con-

fronted by the sight she had just witnessed? In all hon-
esty, Alice Rose asked herself, could this be good for a
young girl? For her moral, spiritual, and educational
development?

Chapter 7

WAS GOD LAUGHING at her? Was He trying to make a cruel joke out of the question she had just asked herself at the *Enterprise* office about her spiritual development? If he was, it wasn't funny.

Alice Rose had nearly bumped smack into Jewel Petty in the lobby of the International Hotel. "And your dear mother would be so pleased, I just know it, Alice Rose, if you would join our Bible class. You know it is so easy to neglect one's moral and spiritual development in a town like this. We must be constantly vigilant."

Vigilant. That word! Ben Warren, the head of the Volunteer Firemen's Association and owner of the Sazerac Saloon, had been complaining just yesterday about the

newly formed Society of Seven, which he said were no
better that a pack of vigilantes looking for a lynching.
They had already accomplished this when they broke into
the jail last spring and strung up Dan Everett; now they'd
gone and cut up a hurdy-gurdy girl. Ben had just put her
on the stagecoach and paid her way back home.

Vigilantism, he called it.

And here was Jewel Petty talking about being vigilant
about spiritual development. The Society of Seven
claimed to be spiritual, too, but all they were doing was
sticking their noses into everyone else's business and
making up rules. Rules about who could sell what on
Sundays and how women should dress in public and how
there should be curfews in Chinatown. Alice Rose just
bet that Jewel's Bible group was into making up rules as
well. No, she wouldn't join that group for all the tea in
China. Besides, her mother had said that people's religion
was their own private business; that you didn't need a
church, a preacher, or a Sunday school class if you were a
true Christian and had Jesus in your heart. Carrie Tucker
had been a true Christian.

Jewel Petty continued talking. "And my darling little

niece Precious has just arrived from St. Louis. I so want you to meet her and for you girls to become good friends.

"Precious! Precious, over here, dear. Alice Rose, this is Precious."

Alice Rose looked at what was in front of her. Precious resembled one of those fancy porcelain dolls. She had sausage curls that framed her face. Her hairdo made her look like an ad for a German butcher shop—kielbasa, knockwurst, bratwurst. She wore a dress that had more supports than the main shaft of the Comstock. Alice Rose bet there were at least three starched layers of petticoats. She had no idea how this sausage-head could walk in such a contraption.

"Precious—is that her name?" Alice Rose asked.

Jewel looked temporarily flustered. She coughed slightly and smiled that tight little smile that Alice Rose hated. "Why, yes, Alice Rose, it is dear." Precious Petty simply stared and pursed her lips a little tighter. For one of the few times in the life of Precious Petty, she had failed to impress someone. Somehow, she seemed to sense this. She looked Alice Rose up and down, head to toe. Alice Rose was suddenly aware of the frayed hem of her skirt and her own scuffy boots.

"I am giving a tea party in honor of Precious next Thursday. I'll send you an invitation. We would love it if you would come. Wouldn't we, Precious?" Jewel Petty said.

"Most certainly," Precious replied, but her eyes were cold and her mouth clamped shut as soon as the two words were out.

"What are you doing here anyway, Alice Rose?" Jewel Petty asked.

"Oh, just going to see a friend."

"Well, I hope you don't have to take the elevator."

"Why?" Alice Rose asked, puzzled.

"Oh, they have a Chinaman running the thing. I declare, this town is getting overrun with the Chinese." She leaned forward. Her face was large and pink with billowing cheeks between which was set a very tiny, babylike mouth. "You know they eat cats, don't you?"

"I thought it was dogs." As far as Alice Rose was concerned, there were too many darned dogs in the town already.

"Cats, too, and they worship dragons!" snapped Jewel. "Poor Miss Griswold lost Purty, that caramel manx."

"How did she know it got eaten?"

"She had hired a Chinaman to work in her garden. She'd seen him eyin' that cat for two days. Third day, the cat disappeared and so did the Chinaman." She paused, then added, "They eat them with noodles."

"How do you know?" Alice Rose asked.

The question seemed to catch Jewel Petty by surprise. "I . . . I . . . ," she stammered. "I just know. My husband—he knows about these things. . . . Oh, there's Mrs. Grumbach. I must invite her to our tea. I'll be right back, Precious." She rushed over to a lady who had just entered the lobby. This left Alice Rose and Precious alone together.

"Auntie said you're an orphan."

"I am not. I have a father."

"She said that he hangs out with a bunch of drinking men and doesn't pay you much thought. That you're growing up wild as an Indian."

"My father works as managing editor of the *Territorial Enterprise*, for your information." Alice Rose paused. "And by the way, if I were you, I would steer clear of Mrs. Grumbach's husband's shop."

"Why's that?"

"He's the German butcher here in Virginia City. And with that mess of pig guts coming out of your scalp he just might mistake you for a walking sausage display and chop off your head."

Alice Rose turned and headed for the elevator.

"Alice Rose!" Hop Sing exclaimed. "I have solution to your problem."

"The godets?"

"Yes. There is fancy lady from Chicago. She wears dress with them. I carry her up and down in elevator at least eight, maybe nine times already. All her dresses have godets. I make a very good study. I see how you do it. I have picture right here in my pocket." He took out a piece of paper.

"This is beautiful, Hop Sing." Alice Rose gasped as she studied the thin lines, so precise, so elegant, the design so clear. "You're an artist."

"Oh, no, Alice Rose. I just see things very clearly. Then can come up with solutions."

"Well, if you're not an artist, you're an engineer." Alice Rose remembered the night in the cemetery and how Hop Sing seemed to be able to see right through the rock. "Could you come over to our place? I got the material and I sure don't want to make any mistakes when I cut it."

"Sure. I come."

So it was arranged. Hop Sing would come over the next evening after work.

Chapter 8

"WHAT IN TARNATION!" Stanley Tucker blinked as he walked through the door of his apartment. There were yards and yards of fabric spread everywhere. Detta Bush stood in the center of the room preening before a mirror that a small Chinese man held in front of her.

"Oh, hi, Dad." Alice spoke through a mouthful of pins.

"You gone into the dressmaking business?"

"Well, I guess you could say that."

"She better say that! Why the heck you think I came back with you?" a big voice shouted. When Buffalo Jo spoke, it always reminded Alice Rose of the steam engines starting up at the ore-crushing mills. Buffalo Jo herself could have crushed a few hunks of quartz. "Your daddy was kind enough to sweet-talk that silly excuse of a deputy out of hauling me off to jail. So then we had a drink or two." Or three, Alice Rose thought. "And I heard Detta was having a fitting over here for some fancy new duds and thought I'd have a look . . . and land's sake, chile . . . that is some rig you done for Detta. How 'bout you make me one?"

Alice Rose had been down on the floor pinning the hem when suddenly Hop Sing was next to her whispering, "More money, big gal Buffalo Jo, more fabric to cover big behind!" Alice Rose started to laugh so hard she thought she might swallow a pin.

"You gotta wait your turn, Jo. After Detta, I promised Eilley Orrum a dress, and it's going to be very complicated."

"I don't want nothin' complicated, Alice Rose, just something pretty that can move with me when I dance." At that Buffalo Jo started jigging around the room. The whole floor creaked, a pitcher on the table trembled. And then, to make matters worse, her father picked up the hurdy-gurdy he'd won in a poker game and began squeezing out a tune and prancing around. Alice Rose hated hurdy-gurdy music. She'd put the squeeze box on her list of most hated musical instruments. It came right before the player piano they had at the Glory Hole saloon. In Boston, her cousins took lessons on a pianoforte. Detta stepped away from Alice Rose and took up the jig. Hop Sing stayed where he was, transfixed by the sight. Alice Rose with her mouth full of pins, just wondered how in the good Lord's name she had wound up here. Why was she in a cramped room with a three-hundred-pound woman, a hurdy-gurdy girl who looked like a painted skeleton, and a father prancing around with a squeeze box?

Why am I here? Alice Rose thought. Why aren't I in Boston with Aunt Eugenia and my dear cousins? She called them dear even though she had never met them, and now she was struck by how pathetic that was. She felt like a beggar on the rim of life with such words.

The thumping of feet, the wheezy sound of the hurdy-gurdy, the shrill shrieks of the dancing girls, all built to a din in Alice Rose's ears. Her head reverberated with the noise. She squeezed her eyes shut. This must be how a dog feels when nasty boys tie tin cans to its tail. Shards of noise clanging in its brain. Why am I here? This is no place for a child! This is no place for a child!

Suddenly, there was no noise. Only the sound of her own voice shrieking *This is no place for a child!* Her father, Buffalo Jo, Detta, and Hop Sing all stood frozen in their places, staring at her. Hop Sing made a gesture toward her. "No!" she cried and tore out of the room.

Chapter 9

THE VIRGINIA CITY DUMP was a favorite spot of Alice Rose's. Some called it the richest dump in the world, as it was absolutely encrusted with champagne corks and oyster shells from all the fancy parties people would give when they struck a vein. And, of course, the International Hotel contributed more than its share.

Alice Rose sat on top of a champagne crate and stared off into the blue haze of the late morning. Amazing what a calming effect the dump always had on her. When she had torn out of the apartment twenty minutes before, crazy with fury and shame, she hardly knew where she was going and could not see through her tears. Her feet just automatically took her to the dump. It was where she always wound up when she was flat-out mad, sad, or stumped. She could think in the dump. She would find a good sitting place and then she could stare off into the blue nothingness of the haze. Or if it was a clear day, with a good squint she could practically pick out every sticker on a cactus in the scrubby desert flats below. In either case, she mostly just fixed her eyes on the barrenness of it all and let her mind fill up.

For Alice Rose, the dump, although hardly a garden spot, defied the ugliness, the scrubbed-out parched emptiness of the land. Here one could browse, find artifacts that confirmed that somewhere out there was a life beyond. *Beyond*, that was the key word. In Virginia City there was really just one dimension—depth, down, underneath. The entire town rested on a thin crust of earth. For beneath the sagebrush-studded slopes, everything had been excavated. The depths now reached more than 600 feet. There had never been mining this deep, and there were more than seventy-five miles of tunnel shafts. Dan De Quille had predicted that within another two years there would be 100 miles, and by the time the decade turned in 1870, there would be close to 200 miles of tunnels! The whole darn town defied gravity. By all rights it should have caved in years ago. Probably would have if Mr. Deidersheimer, the German engineer, hadn't figured out "square sets," the rectangular support systems built out of timbers with which the mines were honeycombed.

But Alice Rose didn't like to think about *down* and *depth*. Two words on her hate list. She liked to think about *beyond*. The champagne crate she sat on came from shippers in New York. There were oyster shells from some distant ocean, a hatbox from a Philadelphia haberdashery, and a cigar box all the way from Havana, Cuba. No cigars in it, but the box was in perfect shape and she meant to take it back with her. All this was practically right at her feet. In another few minutes, when she was feeling more herself, she'd begin her stroll and who knew what goodies she'd find.

But before that, she would do her very next favorite dump thing—blow soap bubbles. Two months ago when she had come out here, right before her mother had given birth to little Perry, she had found a piece of wire with a small hoop on the end. She had remembered once when she was a really little girl back in Golden, Colorado, her mother had fashioned a similar hoop and taught her how to blow soap bubbles. They would sit on the crest of a hill tumbling with wildflowers and blow bubbles. Shimmering like spherical rainbows, the bubbles would drift off toward the snow-covered Rockies. When she found the wire hoop in the dump she ran right home and mixed up a jarful of water and Munyon's Blue laundry soap.

She kept the jar and the wire hoop under a discarded twenty-gallon sugar drum. In some ways, blowing soap bubbles had become more of a ritual than an amusement. And it was one forever entangled with the memory of her mother, the time of apprehension before she gave birth, the terrible fear that plagued Alice Rose during those awful days when her mother was dying, when there was that keen sense of a life slipping out from between her fingers, life leaking away so unstoppably. She had never felt so afraid or so powerless. Some of the women who had come to nurse her mother had tried to send her out to play. How could she think of playing at such a time? But then her mother, in a voice so weak she had to lean over to hear her, said, "Alice Rose, you go out and play. You need to play."

So she had gone, gone to the dump and picked up the

jar of soapy water and the wire hoop. Maybe she had thought that first day if she did things just so, she could stop that leaking life. So she had developed these little rituals. She always approached the sugar drum from the left side and circled it once before taking out the jar. She always carried the jar with both hands and tucked the hoop under her right arm. Even after her mother had died, she continued the ritual.

Now, holding the jar in both her hands, she settled back on the champagne crate, unscrewed the lid, and carefully dipped the hoop in exactly three times before she caught a skin of soapy water. Then with the hoop a few inches from her mouth, she blew very softly. A bubble slowly inflated and began to tremble. With a final short breath and a deft movement of her wrist, the bubble separated from the hoop and began to drift off on the wind. Quickly, she blew another, slightly smaller bubble and then another, a tad bigger. She varied the sizes and never lost one before it floated off the hoop. The idea was to get a whole herd of them floating around. They floated east, to out beyond. They floated over all those prairies where little Tucker babies with flower names lay buried.

They floated on the westerlies that in three or four days would reach Boston, where her cousins attended ice-cream socials and cotillions and read poetry and studied music. They floated away, and in Alice Rose's imagination, they took a little of her with them.

"Quite a sight!" The voice startled Alice Rose so much that she nearly lost the bubble.

"You always go sneaking up on people, Mr. Clemens?"

"Begging your pardon. Didn't mean to give you a start," Sam Clemens replied. "What are you doing out here?"

"Looking for a story, I guess you'd say."

"Girl blowing soap bubbles in the dump. I don't think it'll make much of a story."

"Probably right."

"Of course, there's always stories on the latest petrified rock or piece of wood; everyone's going crazy with them—natural marvels; there were two reports in the *Union* yesterday and one in the *Enterprise* last week. They're common as flies and about as boring."

"Well, yesterday I filled two columns with one wretched hay wagon."

"There was just one?"

"Yep."

"You reported fifteen or sixteen coming in from all directions."

"Just a little multiplication."

"I guess. You got everyone into a fit about hay. Heard people talking about it all over town. I take it, Mr. Clemens, that you aren't . . ." Alice Rose paused as if searching for a word.

"Devoted to the truth? Was that what you were about to say?"

"I suppose so." She cocked her head and gave a little smile.

"In fact, Miss . . ." he hesitated.

"Alice Rose, that's my name."

"Pardon me. I was just going to say that, in fact, Alice Rose, I am a great devotee of the truth. Oh, yes, I sometimes stretch it a bit, but I, for one, will be the first to admit that I do not deal professionally in truth. It is my opinion that too often when people die they have spent up all the truth that is in them and enter the next world as paupers. I plan to be frugal with the truth, so as to save up enough to make an astonishment in the next world."

Alice Rose did not know what to say. She had never in her life heard such a peculiar line of reasoning. Was he serious? It was a very interesting thought—using up truth, or telling lies so as to save the truth. She stood up from the champagne crate. The sun directly overhead fell in sharp, blinding slivers. She had to squint hard to see the figure in front of her. His long red beard was like a cascade of fire. He appeared caught in dazzling cross-beams of glinting light. The contours of his figure became less defined as the edges of his clothing, his shirt, slouch hat, and britches seemed to swim in the waves of heat at high noon.

"Are you trying to tell me you're a liar?"

There was a brief pause and then a nod. "I guess so. Professionally speaking, that is." He paused again and looked at her. "How old are you, Alice Rose?"

"Twelve."

"Would have taken you for at least thirteen or fourteen. You're tall for your age."

"All the children are tall out here."

"That so?"

"Dan De Quille says that they grow tall 'cause there's so little atmospheric pressure."

"That's a new one."

"One of his scientific theories. He makes them up for the most part. He's not exactly devoted to the truth, either. Fact is, none of them are over there at the *Enterprise*. So you'll fit in just fine."

Sam Clemens laughed. "Now where do you fit in, Alice Rose?"

"Not here," she said with a harsh laugh.

"How come you aren't in school?"

"It's not much of a school. Besides, the teacher up and quit last month when Benny Schmitt blew off his thumb during spelling."

"He what?"

"It was the second time it happened in one month. Joe Larrabee blew his off the week before."

"What in tarnation!"

"We got a whole town of thumbless boys around here. They go out and collect old blasting caps from the mines and they think since they're old ones, all the powder is used up, so they start picking around or tapping them or whatever, and even if there's just a trace of powder they can explode. Happens all the time. Boys are so stupid! You'd think they would learn. You don't find one thumbless girl in the whole town, but the boys don't learn," Alice Rose sighed. "Stupid, just plain stupid."

"So that's why the teacher quit?"

"Oh, yes. It makes an unholy mess. Blood spattered all over, bits of flesh and bone. Absolutely ruined three little kids' McGuffy readers. Made a huge ugly splotch on my spelling test. And I had just finished spelling the word *chrysanthemum*. Ever try to spell that word? It's a very hard word to spell, and I did not appreciate having a bloody hunk of Benny Schmitt's finger plopping down in the middle of it!"

"Well, well, well." Sam Clemens spoke softly.

"Yes, that's about all you can say. This wouldn't be happening if I were in Boston going to a proper seminary with my dear cousins and learning proper things."

"Like what?" Sam Clemens asked. She detected a trace of doubt in his voice.

"Like music and poetry and elocution."

"What are you going to elocute about?"

Alice Rose looked at him narrowly. What did he mean? Was he making fun of her? "Anything I want, I suppose." Alice Rose had wanted to say more. She had wanted to say that if she were in Boston she would fit in, but she thought it might sound as if she were bragging. And then something flinched deep inside her—what if she didn't fit in in Boston? She looked out over the scrubby flats of the valley.

"Pretty sight," he said.

"I don't agree," Alice Rose replied tartly.

"You don't? There is something unreachable about it— the colors and so many moods, a kind of wildness."

Alice Rose just grunted.

Sam continued, "Oh, I'll admit it's weird. Kind of unsmiling, I guess you'd say."

"I'd say it's just plain ugly. Nothing pretty about it at all."

"Here you sit in the richest town in America, in what has to be the world's most opulent dump and . . ." he hesitated.

"And I hate it. I know. Strange. I'm the only one who hates this place probably in the whole world."

"Many would think this is the Garden of Eden."

"If you like silver and mining. But I don't."

He chuckled softly. The sun had moved a degree or two from plumb overhead. Sam Clemens's face was no longer wiped out in its blinding light. His greenish eyes twinkled now under his heavily freckled and sunburned brow. "This place is even worse in the winter," Alice Rose added.

"How's that?"

"Well." She sighed deeply. "Come December through end of March there's hardly any light at all in town. Mount Davidson just eats it up. That's why they call it the Suneater. Swallows every morsel of sunshine and casts this big old shadow over the place. The shadow starts creeping in just after midday. It gets darker and darker, creeps across the rooftops up on A Street first. Then it just kind of stretches out and spills over, first onto the sidewalks on the farside of A Street, then the rooftops of B Street." Her voice had a winter chill in it. Her shoulders drooped as she painted in words for him a bleak picture of the richest town in the world glinting in silver but caught in the endless winter shadows.

As she spoke, she realized how much she truly dreaded

the coming winter. Last winter at least her mother had been alive. They made cocoa and her mother read her *Uncle Tom's Cabin*. It was the saddest book ever, but she had felt so warm and cozy and protected. They had wrapped up under a big, thick blanket, and her mother's voice was always so perfect, like a desperate whisper when Eliza sprung from one ice fragment to the next in the swollen roiling waters of the river, to escape the slave hunter. The Civil War was raging and Nevada, not being a state but a territory, was neither Confederate nor Union. The town was split down the middle, and many said the Comstock was just like the baby in the Bible story that King Solomon threatened to cut in two so the parents would each have half. Certainly half the people in this fool town would have been after Eliza. A thought suddenly occurred to her. "Where are you from, Mr. Clemens?"

"Missouri, Hannibal, well, before that, Florida, Missouri. You know when I was born?"

"How would I know that?"

"I guess you wouldn't. November 30, 1835, the same night that Halley's comet streaked across the sky. It only does that once every seventy-five years, you know."

She was impressed: to be born on the same night as a comet appeared over the earth was special. No denying that.

"I plan to go out with Halley's comet."

"You mean die?"

"Yes. It will be the greatest disappointment of my life if I don't go out with Halley's comet. The Almighty has said, no doubt: 'Now here are these two unaccountable freaks of nature, they came in together, they must go out together.'"

"I hope it doesn't come early."

"Me, too."

"If you come from Missouri you must be a Confederate."

"Was for about two weeks."

"How can you be a Confederate for two weeks?"

"Well, I was going to find it harder to be one for life."

"Were you in the army."

"Like I said, for two weeks."

"What happened?"

"Fatigue from constant retreating. Now the Union has a real chance of winning."

Alice Rose chuckled. "But you must have been for slavery."

"No, you got it wrong. I was for Missouri. I am a Missourian, after all. Pro Missouri, against slavery."

"Did your family own slaves?"

"They did. And when I was a child, I must admit I did not know, was never aware, that there was anything wrong with slavery. No one in my hearing said anything against it, not the local papers, my parents, the town fathers. Not even the church. The local church taught us that God approved it. Cited the Bible. 'Course you can cite the Bible and get anything approved."

"How you figure that?" Alice Rose was thinking about Jewel Petty's Bible class.

Sam Clemens sighed. "Can we sit down—I mean long as we're having these lengthy philosophical discussions in the middle of the day."

"Sure," she said. Sam Clemens found another crate. Alice Rose picked up her jar of soap bubbles and screwed on the lid. It wasn't until after Sam began to speak that she remembered that she had not tapped the jar three times on the rim before screwing down the lid. But Sam Clemens could talk like no one she had ever heard. He was like an arroyo after the first hard rains, but instead of great chunks of earth breaking loose and turbulent cascades of roaring water, it was ideas, notions, sentiments, convictions, fancies, impulses, beliefs, views, opinions, all carried on a stream of words. The stream in his southern drawl appeared to meander at a leisurely pace, but underneath was a swift current carrying forth these peculiar and utterly startling ideas.

"The Bible is really just like a drugstore, Alice Rose."

"A drugstore? You don't say."

"I do say. Just like a drugstore. Its contents remain the same, but the medical practice changes."

"You mean whether you're a Presbyterian or a Methodist?"

"Or a Baptist or an Episcopalian or a Catholic. They each treat a headache in a different way and each one swears by the remedy. Now that is not to say that the Bible does not have noble poetry in it and some clever fables and, of course, some really blood-drenched history and some of the best cussin' you can read; there's a veritable wealth of obscenity in the good book." Alice Rose could not think of one curse. Well, maybe in Jeremiah. But nothing as bad as what Benny Schmitt said when he blew off his thumb. "There's some good morals in it, too," Sam Clemens continued. "No complaint there, but there's also upward of a thousand lies."

A thought suddenly occurred to Alice Rose. "Jewel Petty—you know her?" She asked.

"Can't say as I do. Who is she?"

"This real stuck-up lady. She's married to the judge. They put on airs all the time. And she always butts into everyone's business. Anyhow, Jewel Petty is just itching to get her Christian claws into me. She worries about my Christian education, as she puts it, and she wants me to join this stupid Bible class. If you could tell me a real honest-to-gosh Bible lie I might be tempted to join. So tell me a lie, Mr. Clemens. A real Bible whopper." Alice Rose leaned forward eagerly and hugged her knees. She was all ears.

Sam Clemens poked his fingers into his beard and scratched his chin. "Let me cogitate a moment. You want a real fourteen-careat-gold one, right?"

"Right."

"Old Testament or New?"

"I'm not picky—either one."

"Got one! The Bible has told us that during many ages

there were witches. Just read Deuteronomy, chapter eighteen, around verse ten or twelve. Says something to the effect that there aren't to be any daughters that use divination, no hocus-pocus stuff you know. Enchanters, witches, charmers, and wizards are not permitted, and then it goes on to say, 'for all those things are an abomination unto the Lord and that because they are the Lord thy God doth drive them out from before thee.' Now the Bible said 'drive.' I would think just picking those so-called witches up in a stagecoach and depositing them elsewhere would suffice, but no, not for some rabid Bible-toting Christians. They got to burn these charmers! Therefore, the church imprisoned, tortured, hanged, and burned whole hordes of witches, all in the hopes of washing the Christian world clean of their foul blood. Then, lo and behold, it was discovered that there was no such thing as witches, and never has been." He stopped.

Alice Rose was silent. She bit her lip lightly. She had never in her life heard anyone talk this way. She hesitated asking the next question for she remembered what her mother had always said about religion being a private matter and how it was about the rudest thing in the world to go prying into other people's beliefs. Still, she just couldn't help herself, and oddly enough she felt that her mother and Sam Clemens were not that far apart in their religious beliefs. "Are you a Christian, Mr. Clemens? Do you believe in God?"

"Is that one question or two?"

"Well, one, I guess."

"You guess wrong. I am not a Christian if I can help it."

"But if you believe in God you gotta be something," Alice Rose said.

"Says who?" His green eyes were fierce.

"I . . . I . . ." Alice Rose stammered. "I'm not sure."

"The Being who to me is the real God is the One who created this majestic universe and rules it. He is the only originator, the only creator. He is the perfect artisan. The perfect artist. To know God is to know nature. I knew a river once and that is as close as I ever came to knowing God."

"How do you mean you knew a river? What river? And how was it like knowing God?"

"Oh, Alice Rose, you ask hard questions—that's good. But I can't answer them all. The river was the Mississippi.

I was a steamboat pilot. I knew that river by heart. I carried the shape of her in my head, knew every mood and shade of her water."

"And that was God?"

"No. I never said that. I said the closest I ever came to knowing God was knowing a river. I can't explain it. But someday Alice Rose you might find something powerful and mysterious, something of heart-wrenching beauty, and you will want to know it. And you will begin to feel its power and sense its unending mystery, and that will be as close as you get to knowing God."

Alice Rose could not imagine what that something might be. "Then you don't have to be a Christian?"

Sam Clemens pressed his lips together and looked at Alice Rose a long time before answering. "I would say it helps not to be. There has only been one true Christian in the entire history of the earth. Jesus Christ, and they caught and crucified him early." Alice Rose blinked at these words. However, nothing could prepare Alice Rose for what came next. "Furthermore, it is my considered opinion that if Jesus Christ came back to earth right now, there is one thing that he would not be."

"What's that, Mr. Clemens?"

"A Christian."

Alice Rose wanted to say, "You are probably right, Mr. Clemens, but then again there's my mother. I believe that my mother was a Christian." But Alice Rose did not want to say these things outright to Mr. Clemens. Mr. Clemens was a thinking man, and she realized that an adult, perhaps for the first time, was treating her as an equal—a thinking girl or person. She didn't want to just blurt things out. She wanted to think more about what Mr. Clemens was saying, proposing about the nature of the human race. And where did she fit into this scheme of things?

But indeed she had never heard such talk. Alice Rose thought her ears might fall right off. And if there was a God other than the one Sam Clemens referred to, they would certainly be struck dead in the next three seconds.

"Well, I best be going, Mr. Clemens. It's been very interesting talking to you." This had to be the understatement of the century, Alice Rose imagined.

"Same here, Alice Rose. And if you can scare me up a story I would be most appreciative."

"Oh, I'm sure you'll think of something."

"No doubt."

Alice Rose bent over and picked up the jar of Munyons and the wire hoop. She walked back to the sugar drum, tipped it up, and put the jar under. She forgot to approach the drum from the right side as she always did. She forgot to tap it five times before she put it under the drum. She forgot to circle the drum once and then walk off starting off on her left foot, but when she got to the crest of the hill of the dump, she stopped. If Sam Clemens had given her something to think about, she would give him something. She turned around and shouted, "You know, Mr. Clemens, I dare you to write a story about how dag-blasted ugly this stinkhole of a town is. How this country is about as pretty as a singed cat; how this is not by any stretch the Garden of Eden. Why . . . why . . ." Alice Rose searched for the right words. Sam Clemens stood still, transfixed. "Why, Mr. Clemens, it's more like the Devil's spittoon than the Garden of Eden. You write that, Mr. Clemens. I dare you! But for you, 'cause you think it's so pretty, it'll be lying. You'll be saving up some truth for the next world, so you won't be a pauper and can make an astonishment, like you said, when you get there. But I got to tell you, Mr. Clemens, you are a very astonishing man right here on earth. And that is the truth!"

Chapter 10

As Alice Rose walked back into town she happened to look down a back alley behind the Bucket of Blood Saloon. She heard two men arguing. One man's voice was thick with liquor. "I told ya before, I don't cheat at cards. I'm too darned drunk to cheat." It was Mutch arguing with a man in a fancy frock coat. Mutch was right, of course. He was drunk half the time. He always lost at cards. Everyone knew that about Mutch. Perhaps she had better set this stranger straight. Not that she owed Mutch anything. Still, she hated to see an innocent man shot down for something he didn't do. She began to run down the alley. "Hey, mister!" she called. The man turned around slowly. He had a narrow face with a jagged white scar flashing across it like lightning.

"What do you want, little sister?" Darn! She hated when people talked to her this way.

"Mutch is right. He's too drunk to cheat at cards."

"This ain't none of your business, little sister."

"You don't want to go shooting a drunk man who can hardly walk, do you?"

"Little sister, that's enough out of you." The man looked at her coldly. This man was a killer. He just plain wanted to kill Mutch. This wasn't about cards at all. It was about something else. There were cold-eyed killers in Virginia City, men hired to kill—nothing personal, mind you. They were the worst kind of killer there was. Not quick-tempered and fiery-eyed like Johnny Gutt. Their eyes were not just cold, they were dead.

It was a sad fact that children of Virginia City could, if they hung around the back alleys enough, learn to recognize killers the same way children in other places could recognize more common hazards, such as spoiled meat or dangerous swimming holes or rabid dogs.

Alice Rose looked closely at this man's scar, his dead eyes. It might be the killer from Carson City she had heard about. But why was he bothering Mutch? What possible score could anybody have to settle with him?

"You run along, Alice Rose," Mutch said fairly clearly.

Alice Rose turned and ran. She had to find Mr. Clemens. This could be his first big story and he wouldn't have to make up anything. She hightailed it down the alley, turned on to C Street, and ran practically smack dab into Mr. Clemens. Grabbing his hand, she blurted out, "I got a story for you. Follow me." She tugged him along.

"What story?"

"You know that gunslinger, the one got hired to kill that judge over in Carson City?"

"What?"

"You know. And there were all those rumors about him being a spy for the Confederates, and Ben Warren, why he said he wouldn't be surprised if the fellow was in with the Society of Seven, 'cause they hated that judge over there."

"Society of Seven?"

"Oh, Lordy!" burst out Alice Rose. "You don't know who they are? Look, Mr. Clemens, just follow me. I'll explain later. But an innocent man might get hurt."

As they turned into the alley the sound of gunfire cracked the air.

"Mutch!" Alice Rose screamed. But it was too late. "Stop!" she shouted. The man bolted down the far end of the alley where a horse suddenly materialized and he was gone. Alice Rose and Sam stood frozen in their tracks. "We better get to this fellow," Sam said. They ran to where Mutch lay in the dust. His chest heaved and a dark patch of blood bloomed across his shirt. Alice Rose just stared, trying to understand what was happening. The blood looked like the desert poppies that unfurled in early summer.

"This ain't about cards, Alice Rose." The words came out hot and jagged.

"You shouldn't talk, Mutch. Save your breath."

"But it ain't. And she done left to go with me 'cause she loved me . . . Not that preacher man."

"What?"

"She loved . . ." he whispered the words softly, and died.

"Come on, Alice Rose," Sam Clemens said. "This is no place for a young girl."

I know that. That's what I've been trying to tell everyone. But

I'm here, and there's not much I can do about it till I get some money to go back east. So as long as I'm here . . . It was a full half minute before Alice Rose realized that this entire conversation was inside her head, that she had not spoken a word out loud. They were both crouched beside the body of Mutch. She touched Sam Clemens's knee lightly. "Mr. Clemens, I'm here and there's no way that can be changed now. Listen to me. Poor old Mutch was just a sodden old drunk who'd never hurt a flea. Nobody would want to kill him. This really isn't about cards."

"He said it was about love, Alice Rose. And people have killed for love."

"I know, but I don't think that man is the preacher man whose wife Mutch ran off with. And you don't send out someone like him to kill an old drunk who on his one sober day ran off with someone's wife. Did you see how that horse—and it was a good horse—just showed up right on time at the end of the alley?"

"You saying he's got backers, this fella?"

Alice Rose nodded somberly. "Mr. Clemens, this is your first story and it's not about a drunk shot in a back alley."

"So what's it about?"

"I'm not sure." Good Lord, was she going to have to lead this man through every step of the journalistic process? Here she'd delivered him a genuine story.

"What are you thinking, Alice Rose?"

She was about to say, "You're going to have to get off your butt and investigate. You can't just make up lies this time." But she stopped before the first word. "We're going to have to get off our butts and start investigating. This could turn into much more than the run-of-the-mill murder. Those happen everyday. Two drunks kill each other for no good reason. But this is unnatural." And she thought of the lightning flashing across the man's face.

Chapter 11

SAM CLEMENS SAT in a cloud of smoke from his pipe and scribbled some remarks in a small notebook.

> Have met a most peculiar girl. Alice Rose Tucker, the managing editor's daughter. I'm not sure if I should thank her or the murderer, but she seems to have delivered my first real story to me. The murderer escaped before I could fall on my knees and say, "Sir, you are a stranger to me, but you have done me a kindness this day which I can never forget. I was in trouble and you have relieved me nobly and at a time when all seemed dark and drear. Count me your friend from this time forth, for I am not a man to forget a favor." That's what I would say. Alice Rose I thanked in person. Now she feels that this is but the tip of a bloody iceberg. She's talking conspiracy

and promises to be over directly to fill me in on the
details, the background that she feels I need to have
in order to go forth. . . .

At that moment, there was a knock on the door. "Come in!"
he called. Alice Rose entered. "Blaahh!" she made a scalding
sound in the back of her throat. "Can we open a window?"
She did not wait for a reply but, waving her arms to clear
the smoke, made directly for the window. She shoved on
the sash and the window went up. "I think I'll sit right here."
she said, perching herself on the sill. "Air's better." Alice
Rose blinked through the blue swirl of smoke. "Lordy! Mr.
Clemens, you've gone and shaved off your beard!"

"Yes," Sam said, rubbing his bare chin. He still had his
thick, drooping mustache and a nice square angle to his
jaw. He had trimmed his tousled, curly hair, too.

"You look downright decent." Alice Rose clapped her
hand over her mouth and blushed as red as Sam
Clemens's departed beard.

But he merely laughed. "Oh, my lord, I'll have to grow
it again. You know I've got a reputation to keep up."

"I didn't mean it the way it sounded."

"Yes, you did. Don't lie to me, Alice Rose. Remember,

I'm a professional. But you didn't come here to talk about tonsorial matters."

"What are tonsorial matters?"

"Anything to do with hair or whiskers."

"You sure do know a lot of words," Alice Rose remarked.

"Before I came out here I was a printer's devil, laying up type and all."

"I thought you said you were a steamboat man on the Mississippi."

"That, too. But when you work putting type in trays all day you learn a lot of words. You don't just learn them, you touch them, you feel them, you breathe them. You know how to read them upside down and backward. Words just kind of seep right into you." And right out of you, Alice Rose thought, for indeed, she had never heard anyone talk so much or have as many opinions as Sam Clemens.

"All right, now tell me your theory."

"I take it you've not heard of the Society of Seven?"

"Never."

"Well, they're very secret. No one really knows who the members are. But here are some facts: last April, they busted into the jail and got Ed Pike. Pike was rumored to be a Union spy, but he'd also filed a bad claim. That was what got him in jail. The Society of Seven must have thought he was trying to get money out of the Comstock for the Union. The Society of Seven is Confederate, real Copperheads if there ever were any, although they claim they are just a religious society. On God's side, you know. They took Ed Pike out and hanged him. When the coroner cut him down, there was a piece of paper pinned to his body with the number *seven* written on it."

"Didn't anybody see who did it?"

"Well, yes, some people saw, but the men who did it wore black hoods."

"Vigilantes." Sam Clemens spat out the word. "They say that's why the judge was killed down in Carson City."

"How's that? Oh, he was definitely pro-Union, and then again he was soft on a hurdy-gurdy girl who killed some cowpoke in self-defense. The Society hates the hurdy-gurdy girls. You know Gina?"

"Gina?"

"She was one of the prettiest dancers over at the Glory Hole."

"Was?"

"Yes, they just about cut off her nose, a few weeks ago." Alice Rose paused. "And when you were saying out there at the dump about being able to use the Bible to prove anything, well, I couldn't help but think of poor Gina 'cause they pinned some Bible verse to her dress about painted women."

"Christians!"

"Well, they think so." Now Alice Rose said aloud what she had been thinking back at the dump. "See, I don't agree with you entirely, Mr. Clemens. There are some real Christians left. My mother was a real Christian and you got to come with me and meet another, though I think he hardly ever sets foot in a church. He knows more than anybody about the Society of Seven. He's a good man, Ben Warren."

"The fellow who owns the Sazerac saloon?"

Alice Rose nodded.

"Well, any Christian who owns and runs such a fine establishment as the Sazerac cannot be *all* bad."

"He's also the head of the Volunteer Firemen's Association, and they do more good in this town than all the churches put together. They raised money for Gina and sent her back to her parents in New Hampshire. And they'll probably pay for Mutch's funeral."

A quarter of an hour later Alice Rose and Sam Clemens were walking down the wide plank boardwalk and were just about to turn into the swinging doors of the Sazerac, when out of nowhere Precious Petty popped up in front of them. Alice Rose sighed. Was this girl following her or what? It was the third time this week that she had bumped into Precious.

"Oh, hello, Miss Alice Rose. My auntie still wants to know if you'll be coming to Bible class. We have room for one more."

"Well, I am awfully busy these days," Alice Rose replied. "I'm helping Mr. Sam Clemens on a story. Have you met Mr. Clemens? He's the newest reporter on the *Enterprise*. I'm just introducing him around town and showing him the lay of the land, as they say."

Sam Clemens tipped his hat, revealing the fiery wild conflagration that passed for his hair. He extended a large, rough hand. Precious Petty looked as if she would rather touch a rattlesnake, but she timidly extended her own small, white hand. This was the first time Alice Rose had seen Precious alone. "Where is your aunt?" she asked.

"Just down the street at the dry goods store."

"Oh, Alice Rose!" A beautiful lady's head peeked over the swinging doors of the Sazerac. "Girl! We all want to talk to you about these dresses. We hear you're making one for Eilley and one for old Detta at the Flush Times. And they say you do chiffonettes and standout collars and double flounces."

"I'll be right in, Miss Simone. Excuse me, Precious, but Mr. Clemens and I have an appointment with Mr. Warren, the proprietor of the Sazerac. Very nice seeing you."

"You're going in there, Alice Rose?" Precious was in awe. "You make dresses for those . . . those ladies?"

"Sometimes. But I really must go. As you can see Precious, I am awfully busy; so I don't know if I'll have time for Bible class."

"Nice meeting you, Miss Precious." Sam Clemens tipped his hat again, and they entered the saloon.

* * *

The Sazerac was by far and away the best saloon in town. Ben Warren had imported the long mahogany bar from San Francisco. The gaslights hung in sparkling cocoons of colored glass. The brass twinkled, the wood gleamed, and the hurdy-gurdy girls sparkled in all their spangled glory. It was Alice Rose's opinion that this was the way hurdy-gurdy girls should look. The girls at the Sazerac didn't paint up as much because their skin was better, their clothes nicer. And they were the best dancing girls in town. Alice Rose and Sam Clemens made straight for the bar.

"Miss Alice Rose, what can I do for you?" Ben Warren asked.

"One Sissy Sazerac, Mr. Warren." Ben Warren was the handsomest man Alice Rose had ever seen. He had bright blue eyes in a lean face. His dark blond hair fell across his brow in a rakish manner, and his white teeth flashed in a smile from under the drooping mustache. She always felt a storm of butterflies kick up in her chest when she saw him. When she grew up he would be just the kind of man she might want to marry, if she ever married. Of course, by that time, Ben Warren would already be taken and so old it wouldn't matter. He was at least thirty, she bet.

"What's a Sissy Sazerac?" Sam Clemens inquired.

"No bourbon. Just sugar, bitters, and lemon juice. You might want to try one," she suggested, thinking that after all, they were supposed to be working.

"Why, in heaven's name?" Clemens replied. "I'll take the un-sissified Sazerac, if you please."

Ben Warren came back with the drinks. "Have you met Mr. Clemens, Mr. Warren?"

"I have had the pleasure. He's been in here often with your dad and Dan De Quille."

"Well, we're here on business," Alice Rose said, trying not to get too flustered by those blue eyes that sparkled as brightly as the brass.

"What kind of business?"

"Did you hear about Mutch?" Alice Rose asked.

"I just heard it. Who'd ever want to kill that old drunk?"

"Precisely," she replied.

"They didn't catch the fellow?"

"No, but I saw him." Then Alice Rose recounted how she had come across the two men arguing in the alley.

Ben Warren's face darkened. He leaned forward close to Alice Rose and put her hand on top of hers. She thought she might faint.

"How many people know that you saw the killer?"

"Sheriff and his deputy, that's all I think."

"I got to get right over there!" Ben Warren was reaching under the counter for his hat and gun.

"What?" Alice Rose said. "But we haven't finished our questions. We're interviewing you, Mr. Warren. I wanted you to tell Mr. Clemens here about the Society of Seven." Ben Warren shot her a dark look. "And," she couldn't get the words out fast enough, "you don't know what his dying words were—he talked about some woman."

"Alice Rose, shut up!" Ben Warren looked at her fiercely.

She was frozen on the bar stool. The words were like a slap across her face. Sam Clemens was striding out of the bar with Ben Warren. Alice Rose sat dumbfounded with her mouth hanging open. How had this happened? How had it all gone so wrong? And what had happened with Mr. Clemens? He had walked right out with Ben Warren. They were supposed to be a team and investigate this story together. Alice Rose felt so rotten she thought she might throw up.

"Alice Rose, Alice Rose," a voice was calling. It was Juliet Brown.

"Yes?"

"Alice Rose, I hear you're making gowns for Detta and some others over at the Flush Times. I was wondering . . ."

Any other time Alice Rose would have been thrilled to be approached with such a request, but right now, as her shock subsided, a fury was engulfing her.

"Listen, Juliet, I'm in a big hurry. But I'll come back later, I promise." And with that, she hopped off the bar stool and raced down to the sheriff's office.

"Don't you ever tell me to shut up again, Mr. Ben Warren!" she roared as she raced into the office, nearly colliding with a deputy.

"Now calm down, Alice Rose. Just calm down!" Stu, the sheriff, was out of his seat and standing between Alice Rose and Ben Warren. "We know you've been through some trying times lately, losing your mother and all."

Alice Rose set her lips in a firm grim line, her nostrils

flared, and her eyes were half closed with contempt. They were doing it again, treating her like someone's injured pet. Through clenched teeth came her gritty voice. "This has nothing to do with my mother's dying. This is about rudeness!" Her anger flashed. "Mr. Ben Warren, you have no business telling me to shut up. I had brought Mr. Clemens to the Sazerac so you could tell what you know about the Society of Seven. I happened to have been witness to a crime."

"Hold it right there, Alice Rose." Ben Warren's voice had changed completely. There was almost a quaver in it. "Alice Rose." He put his hand to his brow as if he had a headache. "Alice Rose," he began again. "I am truly sorry if I offended you in any way. It's just that, well, sometimes you are too smart for your own good. It is very bad, very dangerous for you that you were a witness to this crime, especially if what I think you think is true."

Suddenly Alice Rose was scared. She had never thought of it this way. She was after all the sole witness; the only person who could identify the killer. "What do you think I think?"

"That there is someone behind this, that a drunk getting killed in this town is hardly news, but that someone sending a hired gun out to get one is unusual. That something just plain doesn't smell right here. But, Alice Rose, the sheriff and I think that the fact that you were an eyewitness can go no further than this room."

"He's right, Alice Rose," Stu broke in. "For the time being, we're going to treat this like any other drunk getting shot by another drunk over nothing. You understand?"

"Yes, I guess."

"Don't guess, Alice Rose. You got to understand this completely. You are in danger. If anyone knows, your life ain't worth a plugged nickel. They'll put you to bed with a pick and shovel if you ain't careful, young lady," the sheriff said. That riled her up again. Lordy, she hated it when people called her young lady. She knew exactly what they were trying to do. Put her in her place. It was an insult disguised as a compliment. She'd rather be just a plain girl.

"All right, I understand, Stu, but kindly do not call me 'young lady.' It does not sit well with me. Just stick to my Christian name." She glared at the sheriff. Ben Warren and Sam Clemens exchanged glances of wonder mixed

with fascination. "And furthermore, even if I am not supposed to own to being a witness in public, I would think
you would be interested in what Mutch said to me about
this woman he claimed to have run off with."

"Yes, yes, we are," Stu said. "The thing I don't get is the
connection to the Society of Seven business. They're
nothing more than a pack of hooded vigilantes. They
never show their face. This fellow, why he's got a more
than memorable face with that scar you described. It's
just not their kind of operation. We know they're pro-
Confederacy, and they've been getting heavy into regulating public morality, but if they'd go after every drunk
in Virginia City they'd use up all their ammunition. It just
doesn't make sense. They play for much higher stakes
than drunks. Unless Mutch had some feet that were going
to pay off."

"No," said Alice Rose. "Those feet of his weren't worth
anything."

She was as stumped as the rest. What Stu had just said
was true. She couldn't figure out why she had jumped to
the conclusion that the Society of Seven was involved,
except for the fact that Ben Warren had said he'd bet they

would like to have a killer working for them like the scar-faced man.

"You have a point, Stu." Ben Warren began to speak thoughtfully. "But supposing the Society doesn't always want to leave the obvious signs of their handiwork? Suppose they're moving beyond their so-called purpose of being mere law-and-order fanatics. Suppose they are turning into first-order criminals themselves."

"But for what reason?"

"The Confederacy needs money. Maybe that preacher's wife had some of her own and gave it to Mutch. Never can tell," Ben Warren said.

"I just can't figure how a common drunk fits into this."

"He was a drunk who was in love with a preacher's wife." Alice Rose spoke almost wistfully. "I never knew Mutch had it in him to love anything like a preacher's wife."

"You sure it was a preacher's wife?" Stu asked, scratching his head.

"Yes, it's true," Sam Clemens broke in. "That is what he said with his dying breath: 'She done left to go with me 'cause she loved me. Not that preacher man.'" He paused and scratched at his chin through his beard. "So maybe we'll have to find out about this preacher man."

He said *we*, Alice Rose thought with delight. She didn't care what they called her now as long as Mr. Clemens said we and meant her and him together investigating this. She'd lie low; she'd never let on to a soul that she had been the witness to the horrible murder of poor old Mutch if only she could help Mr. Clemens.

Chapter 12

Mr. Herr Weisnicht has just arrived in Virginia City from the Humboldt mines and regions beyond. He brings with him the head and the foot of the petrified man, lately found in the mountains near Gravelly Ford. A skillful assayer has analyzed a small portion of dirt found under the nail of the great toe and pronounces the man to have been a native of the Kingdom of New Jersey.

"Shoot!" Alice Rose flung down the paper. This was the second day in a row that Sam Clemens was running with this pure poppycock story about the discovery of a petrified man northeast of Virginia City. The whole article, one absurdity after the next, had been devised to poke fun at the coroner, Justice Sewell, with whom Clemens had a falling out over cards. He wrote that Justice Sewell had concluded that "the deceased came to his death by protracted exposure."

The astounding thing was that most of the readers of the story had accepted it as the truth. Her father had said that Smithy over at a rival newspaper in Carson City wanted to run it. Even though he knew it was poppy-cock, he thought it was about the funniest thing he had ever read. Her dad predicted that every newspaper in the West would pick up the story. So here was Sam Clemens off and running, telling lies as fast as he could spin them and, of course, saving up the truth for his appearance in heaven. In the meantime, Alice Rose, who wanted to get to the bottom of Mutch's murder, seemed to be frus-trated every step of the way. "Shoot!" she muttered again. "He should be a novelist, not a journalist."

Alice Rose sighed and looked about the small apart-ment. It seemed crowded now, blooming with fancy dresses in various stages of finish. It had been almost a month since she had completed Detta's dress. Now she had several orders from the girls at the Sazerac and another two for girls from Detta's saloon. An immense cloud of lavender lustring, a kind of silk, hung from the ceiling's gaslight fixture. She was starting the ruffle work on it for Buffalo Jo. It looked more like a thunderhead in July than a dancing dress. And she had finally just finished Eilley Orrum's dress with the godets. Mr. Clemens, who had been wanting to meet Eilley and see her mansion, had agreed to rent a buckboard from the city stables and give her a ride out.

Suddenly there was a boom, and the dress overhead began to shake on the end of its gaslight tether. The blasting had increased twofold in the past month. Miners were driving shafts into Mount Davidson deeper than anyone had ever imagined. Track was being laid for ore cars on the incline shafts that followed the rich silver veins into the earth at the rate of a quarter mile a week. The steep slopes of the mountain bristled with the headworks buildings of the mines, which housed the gears, the reels of cable, and the steam-driven hoisting equipment, or the "donkey engines" that hauled the ore cars up and down the shaft. There was the constant thrum of the engines, mingled with the nearly incessant booming of the underground blasting.

More and more investors flocked in from San Francisco, and the more money that came into the town, the more was spent at the saloons and fine hotels. The sidewalks swelled with people, and streets were clogged with quartz wagons. Every hurdy-gurdy girl was enjoying the benefits of these flush times, and Alice Rose was getting her fair share as they flocked to her to get themselves fancy new rigs.

Alice Rose knew she should be happy. If her business continued like this, she figured she would have enough money by this time next year to take the stage back East. But the murder of Mutch had distracted her from thoughts of the East. The man with the lightning scar flashing down his face had started to haunt her dreams. There was a knock at the door.

"Hop Sing!" she called out.

"Yes, it's me, Alice Rose." She opened the door. "I not late?"

"No. Mr. Clemens is late, as usual."

"You got dress packed up for Miss Eilley?"

"Yes, right over there." She pointed to a large box tied with twine.

"Alice Rose, I got a deal I want to make with you."

"What's that, Hop Sing?"

He drew a mine claim form from the deep pocket of his baggy pants. Alice Rose couldn't imagine what he was doing with a mine claim form. The Chinese were not allowed to hold claims. In fact, the Chinese were not even permitted to work in the mines. Nor were they permitted to give testimony in a court or send their children to school. "Where did you ever get that?" Alice Rose asked.

"Never you mind that, Miss Alice Rose."

"But you know the law. I can't fill it out for you, Hop Sing."

"You fill it out for yourself."

"I don't give a hoot about mining and silver, Hop Sing."

"Yes, but I do. We become partners. I am your silent, invisible partner. You fill out the claim in your name, then we split fifty-fifty. Come on, Alice Rose, you might get rich." Although there were laws forbidding Chinese from holding claims, there were no laws forbidding minors. Hop Sing had been so helpful to Alice Rose it seemed wrong to refuse him this simple request. "Come on, Alice Rose, we be partners." She remembered how much she had wanted to be Mr. Clemens's partner in solving Mutch's murder and helping him to write the truth. "Okay, Hop Sing. I'll file this claim. But we better write down what's between you and me, don't you think?"

"No, I trust you Alice Rose, you trust me. We shake hands." With that, he thrust out his slender hand. Alice Rose took it firmly and they shook. It felt good.

"Alice Rose! Alice Rose!" A voice called from outside. There was another boom and the room shook. Alice Rose went to the window and pushed it open. Leaning out, she saw Sam Clemens waiting for her in the buckboard. "Be right down, Mr. Clemens. Hop Sing is coming with us."

"All right. Don't dally."

Alice Rose made a face. Imagine *him* telling *her* not to dally. That was practically all Sam Clemens did as far as she could see. She had to admit, however, that she did enjoy his company.

Alice Rose took her duster off the wall hook and put it over her dress. It didn't pay to go out without it on these late autumn days. It was the season of the Washoe zephyrs. These strong and sudden gusts out of the west would crash into Mount Davidson, tumble over its crest sweeping down furious wind gales that do-si-doed around the town, picking up stray cats and the occasional dog, snatching hats and lifting tin roofs before depositing a bounty of dust over everything.

When they came downstairs, just as they were about to get in the buckboard, who should come along but Precious Petty. She was strolling down the wide wood plank sidewalk, her sausage curls perfect despite the wind. She was accompanied by her uncle, Judge Horace Petty.

"Well, hello, Miss Alice Rose," Judge Petty said.

"Hello, Judge." Alice Rose stopped before climbing up into the buckboard. She didn't want to appear rude to the judge. She respected the law, even if she'd didn't respect his niece and her stupid sausage curls. "Where are you off to?" asked Precious.

"Oh, to Eilley Orrum's. I'm doing some dressmaking for her."

"And who's your friend?" the judge asked, nodding toward Sam Clemens.

"Oh, this is Mr. Clemens," Alice Rose said, and then by

way of further introduction, added, "one of the boys from the *Enterprise*. Wants to meet Eilley."

"Boys?" asked Precious.

"Oh, they're grown-up men, but I just call them boys 'cause they so foolish sometimes." Alice Rose shrugged in what she felt was a nonchalant, very grown-up way.

Judge Petty laughed. "You're right, Alice Rose, that you are! You do a good job of looking after that whole lot, including your daddy."

Precious stared openly at Alice Rose as if she were seeing something quite strange. "Well, I better be on my way," Alice Rose said.

As she climbed up beside Mr. Clemens she felt Precious's eyes boring into her back. "What she got on her feet, Uncle?" she heard Precious ask.

"Oh, probably Indian moccasins. They say they keep your feet cool in heat and warm in cold."

Alice Rose later realized that both Precious and her uncle seemed not to see Hop Sing at all. They were simply blind to his presence.

The sky was a flawless blue as they drove out of town. The mountain had not yet swallowed the sun, and Alice

Rose tipped her face upward to catch the strong rays. If she could only store them against the coming darkness of the long winter days. She sighed.

"You seem mighty peaceful, Alice Rose," Sam Clemens commented.

"Ummm, maybe I'm petrified."

"Hah! Can you beat it. Who would have ever thought people would believe that roaring string of absurdities, but they swallowed it whole. Here I had set out to make fun of all this petrifaction business you been telling me about, and this marvelous creature I created just for fun is exalted and glorified. A curious miscarriage of my theme I would say."

"A curious distraction from our business at hand," Alice Rose replied.

"What business is that, Alice Rose?" Hop Sing asked.

"Mutch's murder, I—" Sam Clemens gave her a sharp jab in the ribs with his elbow. Alice Rose had forgotten. No one was supposed to know that she had been a witness. But she trusted Hop Sing. "There's just a rumor floating about that before he died, Mutch had run off with somebody's woman."

"Ah yes, I know this. Preacher's wife."

Alice Rose and Sam Clemens both swung their heads around at the same time toward Hop Sing, who was sitting next to Alice Rose, at the end of the buckboard seat.

"How?" they both said at once.

"I told you, Alice Rose, I came from Carson City, before here. You hear things. Gossip, you know."

"Why did she run off, especially with Mutch?" Alice Rose asked.

"Reverend Jessup, that was her husband, everyone says he was an old and cranky fellow. Mutch, he was nice when sober and more good-looking than Reverend Jessup."

"That's hard to believe," Alice Rose said.

"He's pretty ugly, Reverend Jessup."

"Hey, he doesn't have a white scar flashing down his cheek like lightning, does he?" Sam Clemens gave Alice Rose another jab in her ribs.

"Oh, no. That the guy they say killed Judge Claymore over in Carson City," Hop Sing said. "Not a nice man. Want to stay way from him."

There seemed to be a lot of people to stay away from,

Alice Rose thought. Well, she didn't want to think about that right now. It was a clear, lovely day and she meant to enjoy the sunshine as best she could. In another few weeks there could be snow covering the whole place, and all one would see would be the stovepipes sticking out of the coyote holes. The coyote holes were dug as shelters by miners who could not afford the price of a room in town. Dan De Quille said that in the winter Mount Davidson looked like a man's head smoking a hundred pipes because of the coyote holes.

Chapter 13

ALICE ROSE AND SAM CLEMENS stood in the south parlor of Eilley's mansion. It was decorated with plush velvet curtains and thick carpets with glistening gold fringe. "So that's her!" Sam Clemens nodded at the portrait that hung by a small arched doorway.

"Yes,"Alice Rose replied.

"Those real?" Sam Clemens asked, walking up to a walnut table with a huge silver bowl spilling with ivy and purple grapes.

"No, wax. Eilley has a passion for grapes. She has them carved on her headboard and painted on the walls. It was a notion she picked up in Europe on her Grand Tour."

"Doesn't have grapes up there," Sam said tipping his head back to look at the ceiling.

"No, naked ladies instead. Well, almost naked. She had the painter put in the clouds to keep them proper. It's a scene from mythology. She even borrowed a book of my mother's for the painter to copy. It's Diana, the goddess of hunting, and her assistants. They're called nymphs, the assistants."

"You don't say. Very impressive." Sam took out his notebook and began writing. Just then, from the smaller room through the door, they heard Eilley's voice, loud and fretting.

"Hang it, Drake! They're trying to get at the number fifty-two vein and hold it hostage for the Confederacy. That's all they're doing and you know it plain as the nose on your face. You seen those stone forts Carter's been setting, Andy? They are nothing more than command posts along the Comstock Lode. He wants to claim the whole mountain as a war prize for the Confederacy. He's no simple lawyer, that Carter. He wants to be a general. He's got his soldiers out here on watch. He's going to monitor every darned claim and every shaft. Why I declare, he's probably picturing the last decisive battle of the war being fought out here in Nevada—a territory, not even a state! Can you beat that?"

"Of course, I know this, Eilley," Drake replied. Eilley Orrum and Andy Drake came striding into the room. Drake was a tall, imposing man with a long blond beard bright as gold. He was well known around Virginia City as an honest, tough lawyer who always packed twin navy derringers in his frock coat. He'd been educated at Harvard, specializing in mining disputes, and was definitely on the Union side. He had made as much money as some of the richest miners from their lucky strikes. His archenemy was Willy Carter, a former Texas Ranger, whose elegant manners camouflaged a rough and violent nature. He was not a man to toy with. Now he was going after Eilley Orrum's central lead number fifty-two which produced well over two million dollars a year in silver.

"Oh, Alice Rose! I completely forgot, today's delivery day, isn't it?" Eilley said.

"Yes, ma'am. This is my friend Sam Clemens who wants to meet you, and this is Hop Sing."

"Oh, I know Hop Sing. He fixed up one of my old arastras at the crushing mill. Made a clever little gear gizmo."

"Well, he helped me with those godets, too."

"You're worth your weight in silver!" Eilley exclaimed

to a beaming Hop Sing. She then walked over to Sam Clemens and they shook hands. "Pleased to meet you, Mr. Clemens. Been hearing about you."

"Hope all good."

"Well, not really, seeing as you hang around with all those reprobates from the *Enterprise*. What can you expect!" She laughed heartily. "'Course they're better company than Carter and his gang, that scum."

"Society of Seven?" Alice broke in. "What are they doing to you?"

"Carter's their lawyer. He's representing them. 'Course they don't come right out and say that they're the Society of Seven. They've gone and made up some phony company. Calling it the Rodham Mining Company."

"Well, now, Eilley," Andy Drake broke in, "Their incorporation papers are all in order, quite legal and all."

"That might be, but you and I both know that Rodham Mining Company is just a front for the Society of Seven, Andy."

"What do they want?" Alice Rose asked.

"They're just after fifty feet of central lead fifty-two,

that's all!" Eilley's voice was low and menacing. "They
aren't just regulating public morals anymore and spout-
ing their own kind of religous claptrap. They're showing
their hand now—they want money! The whole lot of
them are just a bunch of secessionists. You know that,
Andy. You know what Carter did last year with the lead
that fellow from California—what's his name? Hearst,
that's it. Mr. Hearst, he had bought some good feet up
there. And Carter sent in those bully boys from his forts
and tried to run the Hearst men right off Hearst's own
property."

"Well, he's not doing that to you."

"No, he's taking me to court instead."

"What's happening—they claiming there's another
ledge coming in there?" Sam Clemens asked.

"Exactly." Both Eilley and Drake answered at once.

"I noticed," Sam Clemens continued, "that since I've
been here, those forts of Carter's look as if they are
stretching now all the way from Gold to Six-mile
Canyon."

"You betcha," Eilley snapped. "He's holding the whole
darned Comstock hostage to the Confederacy—or at

least wants to. You're a Southerner, Mr. Clemens. Which side do you set on?"

Alice Rose wondered if he'd tell the same story that he had told her or perhaps make up a new one. Sometimes adults did that: told one version of a story for children, another for grown-ups. It irritated her. Sam Clemens took in a deep breath. "As I was explaining to Alice Rose the other day, while we were taking the air in the dump, I fought for the Confederacy for exactly two weeks but retired from that occupation due to the fatigue of constant retreating. Anyway, quite frankly the darned uncertainty of this city is killing me. I hate indecision."

Eilley and Drake just stared at him. "You got to get used to Mr. Clemens," Alice Rose offered. "He means no harm. He hardly ever tells the truth, but what he just said might have been."

"Well, I hope you're going to write the truth about this, Mr. Clemens. Willy Carter is behind the whole thing. The Society of Seven was just a ragtag bunch of vigilantes; but once Carter got hold of them, he fashioned them into something else. They're getting to be real professionals. He's turning that hogswill into killers, and they're for the Confederacy. You'll see."

"Don't go writing anything yet, Mr. Clemens." Drake held up a cautionary hand. "I need time to get my case together. I got a plan and I don't want to tip my hand to anyone. We'll win this case, if it does come to court, Eilley. Just keep yourself calm."

"All right, now you hustle along and go about winning my case," Eilley said. "I got other business here with Miss Alice Rose."

"Well, if you don't beat Mr. Gagelin at his own game, Alice Rose Tucker." As Eilley emerged from her boudoir and did a slow turn in front of her oval-shaped mirror, Sam Clemens gave a low appreciative whistle. The skirt of rose silk was looped up in two places in front and two in the back by blue and white ribbons with flattened rosettes. The front had an overlay of white lace ending a few inches short of the hem. The godets set perfectly in the main skirt and added a flare to the hem. Eilley twirled, admiring her image in the mirror.

"Hold it! Hold it, Miss Eilley," Hop Sing cried out. "Let me just fix one thing." He knelt at the hem with a small scissors and quickly trimmed off a trailing piece of thread.

"You two should go into business together!" Eilley exclaimed. "What a team!" Hop Sing winked at Alice Rose. It did seem to Alice Rose that although she was short on parents, she was getting long on business associates: criminal investigating with Mr. Clemens, fashion designing, and mining with Hop Sing.

Chapter 14

THEY SAW THE SMOKE long before they reached Virginia City, curling up black as tar into the startlingly blue sky on this clear November day.

"Must be a mine fire burst out the top through headworks!" Mr. Clemens said.

There were many ways to die in a mine, but no accident was worse, more dreaded, than a mine fire. Cave-ins of timbers, rocks, and earth; unplanned-for explosions, runaway mine cars that crashed into the bottom of shafts, frequently tearing off heads and arms and legs of men, could not compare to the living hell of a mine fire that gulped air and lives. It was always at the points of escape that the fires raged the worst, taunting the trapped victims with the lure of freedom and the certainty of their impending, fiery doom.

But as Alice Rose, Sam Clemens, and Hop Sing approached, they did not smell the familiar sulfurous odors of the earth's burning innards. Suddenly Hop Sing was standing straight up in the buckboard.

"It's Chinatown!" Hop Sing's cry seared the air. "Chinatown is burning!"

Sam Clemens slapped the reins on the back of the horses and they tore off toward the blaze. The smoke was quickly engulfing the whole town. By the time they got there, members of the Volunteer Firemen's Association were surrounding the few blocks in the east end of Virginia City, below D Street. Fire wagons had pulled up, and Alice Rose spotted Ben Warren, his face black with soot, his eyes red. He was carrying a bundle in his arms, small enough it seemed to Alice Rose to be a young child, but in fact it was a very old frail Chinese woman. Hop Sing was out of the wagon before it stopped. Sam Clemens handed the reins to Alice Rose. "Can you drive this rig?"

"Sure."

"Take it back to the livery stable. They need all the help they can get down here. I'm joining a bucket brigade."

Alice Rose drove the buckboard back. She saw her father running the other way with Dan De Quille and Rollin Daggett to join the firemen.

Within twenty minutes she was back in Chinatown and helping. The heat of the fire was tremendous and rushed out at her like a wall. "They need wet blankets on those rooftops over there!" It was Joe Goodman from the *Enterprise*. Alice Rose found a line of people, mostly Chinese women and children, who were waiting to be handed wet blankets to spread on rooftops. A small boy, no more than seven or eight years old, stood in front of Alice Rose. When they piled a drenched blanket into her arms, she could not believe how heavy it was. How had that little boy not staggered under the weight? She followed him through a cut between the houses. Here they handed their blankets down a chain of people who were spreading them onto the roofs. The roofs were below where the people stood, since the town was built on a hillside.

Alice must have carried twenty blankets. She thought her arms would break. But the little boy she had been following never seemed to flag. She wanted to ask him how he did it, but he was so intent on his work, and she was not sure he even spoke English. Then a burly man came up to them and spewed a torrent of Chinese. The little boy turned to Alice Rose and said, "We go to rooftops now. It's our turn to spread blankets."

For the next hour they spread blankets, working their way down the rooftops. On some of the roofs they had to stomp out live sizzling coals. Then suddenly, in the midst of spreading a blanket, the little boy stopped and looked straight out. His eyes filled with tears.

"What's wrong, little boy?" Alice Rose asked.

"My mummy!" He pointed to some men in the street below. Alice Rose took the little boy's hand and they walked to the edge of the roof. The men were carrying out a body wrapped in a bright yellow silk cloth. "That's your mommy?" The little boy nodded solemnly.

"How can you be sure?"

He just shook his head. "You can't be sure," Alice Rose insisted.

"No, I sure. I thought I saw her ghost before when we were carrying the blankets. I thought maybe mistake. Maybe Wu Chow's auntie. But no, my mummy. I got to go now."

"What?" Alice Rose was confused. "Where are you going?"

"I go back to China. I got to take Mummy back to China. I promise her. My father died last year. Now I take them both back to China. No more this stinking America." And with that, he left. He seemed to simply dissolve into the smoke and the throngs of people.

Alice Rose never learned his name and never saw him again for the rest of her life.

She kept spreading blankets until the last roof in the block was covered. When she had finally left the scene, when they said the fire was under control, she headed up an alley toward C Street. It was blocked, however, by the most enormous pile of kindling she had ever seen. As she drew closer, something struck her as odd about it. Then she gasped as she caught sight of a blackened hand reaching stiffly out of the middle of the pile. One by one, charred faces, their mouths drawn back in lipless death grins, stared out from the heap. She felt her stomach turn, but she forced herself to look for the yellow silk in which the little boy's mother had been wrapped. Finally she couldn't take it any longer. She turned and rushed out the alley straight into her father. He put his arms around her. "You get along home, A. R. This is no place for you. The work's almost done. You did a good job up there on the roofs."

"You saw me, Dad?"

"I saw you, Alice Rose. Your mother would have been proud."

"Oh, Daddy! So many died." She leaned her head against his chest, but no tears would come.

"Go along. Get home. I'll be late. I'll have to go back to the office. It'll take the rest of the night to put this story to bed."

Alice Rose wearily climbed the steps to their apartment and opened the door. She went directly over to the washstand, looked in the small mirror above the heavy white porcelain bowl. Her face was dark with soot. She leaned forward and peered harder into the mirror. Beneath the soot, something had happened to her face. She had, in some way, been transfigured by this fire. She took the pitcher and poured some water into the bowl. She

splashed some on her face and took a sliver of soap. She
had to remember to buy some new soap. Her father
never remembered things like that. Then she began to
sob. "This is no place for a child. This is no place for a
child. There is no one to buy soap and keep a proper
home; they stack up dead people like cord wood!" She
reached for a towel and wiped off her face and went to
the windowsill. The bloodred sun sank, turning the
clouds to rubies, and against this ruby sky ashes fluttered.
Then Alice Rose blinked. Something white was falling
right outside the window pane. Snow! How could there
be snow falling over this singed town? But large, fluffy
flakes of snow were swirling over the Sierras to the west
and mingling with the ashes and cinders that floated lazily
in the chill air. For the next five minutes Alice Rose
observed with fascination this bizarre kaleidoscope of
black ash, white flakes, and ruby-red light. And then, like
a giant candle snuffer, Mount Davidson swallowed the
sun and it was completely black outside except for white
snowflakes that still fell slowly.

Alice Rose went to bed. She knew what these blizzards
could be like. By tomorrow the scene of the fire might be

completely covered with a thick blanket of snow. A stranger would come into town and never know of the terrible destruction, the scores of people who had died in Chinatown. It didn't seem quite fair that something so terrible could be so easily wiped out. The last thing she thought about before sleep over took her completely was the little boy. He said he was going home to China. How would he ever do that all by himself? It was hard enough for her to earn the money to go to Boston, which was a lot closer, and she was a lot older. He was a complete orphan; she was just a half orphan. But the little boy had simply vanished, like one of the embers from the fire, the glow quenched in the long dark and snowy night. And she, Alice Rose, was still here in this godforsaken town.

She was drifting on that borderline between dreaming and waking, so she was not sure if the footsteps were part of a dream or from somewhere else. But soon there was a pounding on her door. "Alice Rose! Alice Rose! Wake up! Open up!"

Fire! That was all she could think of, fire! Her limbs were so heavy she could not move them. She saw her arm turning black, the skin charring, white bone protruding. She must get out of here! She must! Finally, she wrenched herself from the last clasping tentacles of sleep, and tearing herself from its deep grip, sat up startled but alert in her bed. Someone was pounding on her door. "Alice Rose. It's me, Sam Clemens." She looked across the room to the alcove where her father slept. The bed was empty. She climbed out from under the warm covers. The wood was like ice on her bare feet. "I'm coming! I'm coming." She glanced at the clock—2:30 in the morning. She opened the door. Sam Clemens looked about as terrible as she had ever seen a man look. His eyes were two dark smudges. His mouth was twisted into an anguished grimace. His shoulders sagged. This man was not merely tired. He was wasted—wasted with some terrible grief.

"Alice Rose," his voice croaked. "Remember that Bible class you were telling me about?"

Alice Rose nodded. "Yes." The whispered word was like a small feather floating in the night. What in the world was he getting at?

"Alice Rose, it's time for you to go to Bible class."

"What?" There was some connection here that she was not making.

"There was some sort of Bible verse scrawled on a door in Chinatown. People are beginning to suspect that some of the most upright 'Christian' members of this community are behind all this. That fire in Chinatown tonight—it was set."

"Set!"

Sam Clemens nodded his big shaggy head. "And we have it on good authority it was set by the Society of Seven."

Alice Rose blinked. "Is that true, Mr. Clemens?"

"Yes, it's true, and not only that. I also heard that if this case of Eilley's really does go to trial it will go into Judge Petty's courtrom."

"So?" Alice Rose waited.

"So, I just found out he's a member of the Society of Seven."

Alice Rose bit her lip lightly. "And that's why you want me to go to Bible class."

"I think it might prove helpful, Alice Rose. You know I, of all people, would never subject a person to Bible class.

Rather see them polka with an alligator, but . . ."

"They're cropping up all over the place, aren't they—the Society of Seven folks?"

"They certainly are. Thicker than flies on a fresh corpse, these Christians."

Chapter 15

THE SMELL OF BAKING COOKIES swirled through the entire house. "Finish up your projects, children." Jewel Petty's voice trilled out above the happy jabber of the seven girls. They were gathered around the work table, putting the finishing touches on their Christmas boxes that the church planned to distribute to the needy that evening. This was Alice Rose's third Bible class. Alice Rose liked the craft and cookie part of the Bible class the best. She didn't mind rolling bandages for the soldiers at the battlefront. Jewel Petty was careful to explain that they were rolling them for the wounded of both the Union and the Confederacy. But Alice Rose had a feeling deep in her gut that these were going to the Confederacy after what Sam Clemens had told her. Still, she rolled and she sewed and she glued and she pasted and she listened to the Bible discussions, which she found infinitely boring. So far all this effort had brought forth nothing. Not a clue, not a shred of information that could help link the Society of Seven to the tragedy of Chinatown or to the murder of Mutch.

Oddly enough, the least difficult part to bear was Precious Petty herself. Precious was drawn to Alice Rose like a moth to a flame. She had sought Alice Rose out on several occasions, waiting for her by the building where Alice Rose and her father lived or on the steps of the *Enterprise* which was near her uncle's law office. Precious liked Alice Rose's stories of the thumbless boys and all the mining towns she had lived in and how she managed for just her father and herself. Of course, Alice Rose had sworn her never to tell her aunt Jewel about the dresses that she made for the hurdy-gurdy girls, but Precious was in awe of Alice Rose's sewing talents. Alice Rose pretended to like Precious. It was all part of the research, the investigation. Pretending to like her was not all that difficult. It was, after all, hard to hate somebody who so completely admired you.

Jewel Petty now settled her soft bunchy figure into the rocking chair. She reached for the Bible on the table beside her and then from a deep pocket took out her spectacles case. She always did these movements with great deliberation. There was a slow rhythmic pace to each gesture. The chatter of the girls ebbed away as they reached into their carrying bags for their Bibles. She now looked over the gold rims of the spectacles. "So nice to see you all here, especially you, dear Alice. My seven little angels.

"Noah and his Sons," she intoned. "'Genesis, Chapter nine. These are the three sons of Noah and of them was the whole earth overspread. And Noah began to be a husbandman and he planted a vineyard: And he drank of the wine, and was drunk. . . .'" A crease furrowed between Jewel Petty's brow. She was doubtlessly thinking about the Glory Hole or the Sazerac, where Alice Rose's father might be at this very moment, probably along with a few of the other girls' fathers as well. Jewel Petty droned on. Alice Rose half listened. Seemed old Noah was so drunk he fell asleep stark naked. His sons Shem and Japeth took a cloth and covered him up. They were very proper about the whole thing and backed up, and just more or less dropped the cloth, so they wouldn't have to see their father bare-butt naked, but Ham, the other son, saw his father and this really set the old man off. "'A curse on Canaan!'" That was the country of his son Ham. "'The lowest of slaves shall he be to his brother. . . . Blessed be Yaweh, the God of Shem. Let Canaan be slaves to others. May God make room for Japheth, That he dwell among the tents of Shem. And let Canaan be their slave.'"

Alice Rose stifled a yawn. Lordy, Mr. Clemens was sure right about one thing. You could use the Bible for just about anything you wanted, from explaining away slavery to burning up witches. There was hardly ever a Bible class without something about how God said slavery was just fine and dandy. Last week it had been First Corinthians, chapter seven: "Let every man abide in the same calling wherein he was called." Then Jewel Petty had gone on and read the verse that said if one was called to be a servant and didn't like it, well too bad. According to St. Paul, God says stick it out!

Alice Rose bent her head and was flipping discreetly through the Bible not looking for anything in particular.

Just ambling along as Mr. Clemens might. She got to Revelations and began to read. There certainly were a lot of numbers mentioned, especially the number *seven*. To seven churches John was to bring the word and there were seven golden candlesticks, seven lamps, seven seals, something about the mystery of the seven stars. She read on in Revelations and reached chapter eight. The words jumped out at her. Seven angels! With seven trumpets. A cold feeling began to crawl over Alice Rose. She looked up at Jewel Petty, who continued to read, the lower rims of the spectacles resting on the little pillows of flesh underneath her eyes. It was Jewel Petty who had called them the seven angels. She tried to collect herself and looked back down at the Bible. The pages were jumping with sevens, seven spirits, seven lamps. The Society of Seven. Was this it? Had she really crawled into the belly of the beast? They had gone on rumors and hunches until now, but was this really it? She looked around at the faces of the other girls. Their parents were doctors and store-keepers and bankers and mine owners. Were all of their folks members of the society? And was this not really a class in Bible stories at all but something else—an attempt maybe to worm into their young brains and plant the seeds of the particular brand of hatred that was a specialty of the Society of Seven? She had heard of Christian love, but was this a class in Christian hatred? Mr. Clemens had wanted her to go to Bible class because he said that there had been reason to believe that the Society of Seven was somehow connected with the Chinatown fire. There had been a Bible phrase about God's wrath scrawled on the charred sign of the Cave of the Dragon Sleepers, an opium den. Jewel Petty had finished the Noah story and was now into Psalms. That meant the class was coming to a close. They always finished with Psalms. But Alice Rose kept reading Revelations and paid no heed to Jewel Petty. The first angel was now opening the first of the seven vials "and poured out his vial upon the earth; and there fell a noisome and grievous sore upon the men which had the mark of the beast and upon them which worshiped his image." Alice Rose looked up and she saw before her not a well-upholstered middle-aged lady in a rocking chair reading the Bible, but a beast, and the beast was speaking: "'Thou shalt tread upon the lion and adder; the young lion and the dragon shalt thou trample under feet.'" The words of the Psalms became inextricably intertwined with other words from another time not too long before. "And you know they eat cats . . . eat cats and worship dragons." All these words were spoken by Jewel Petty. And who had God's wrath swallowed, thought Alice Rose? The image was as vivid as it had been on the day of the fire. The little boy on the edge of the roof, looking down upon the bright piece of yellow silk that wrapped the body of his mother. Alice Rose knew she could not stay in the room a minute longer.

Chapter 16

SHE HAD MADE HER EXCUSES at the end of the reading, claiming a terrible headache. Jewel Petty's words from weeks before about dragon worshipers and cat eaters rang in Alice Rose's ears as she pounded her way down A Street to the corner of A and Sutton.

"Alice Rose! Alice Rose! Wait up!" She stopped and turned around. The snow was fairly deep, and if Precious Petty, all bundled up in her fur-trimmed gray velvet coat, didn't look like a snowshoe rabbit, Alice Rose didn't know what did.

"What are you doing out here, Precious? Somebody's going to take you for a rabbit and shoot you."

"Oh, Alice Rose, you are so funny." Precious's eyes shone with admiration. "I thought you were heading home. Why are you here at Sutton? You live in the other direction."

Alice Rose didn't know what to say. In truth, when she had left, she thought she was heading home, but somehow her feet took her in the direction of Chinatown. This was not the first time she had gone to look for the little boy. She had this compulsion; it was almost a hunger to find him again. In Alice Rose's mind, she and the little boy were linked. They had both been made orphans to a certain degree by this town. She knew it was wrong, maybe, to blame a town, but still, facts were facts. She admired that little boy for getting out. Half of her wanted to find him, but the other half didn't. She wanted to think that he had indeed escaped. But how could she tell all of this to Precious? She was so confused. And worse, she was no closer to untangling the weird web of horror that had begun with the murder of Mutch in that back alley.

"Where are you going Alice Rose?"

"I . . . I . . ." she stammered. "I can't tell you, Precious."

"Alice Rose, I want to be your friend." Precious leaned forward and took one of Alice Rose's hands. Her clear blue eyes fringed with long dark-blond lashes peered into Alice Rose's face. Her eyes brimmed with intensity. She really does want to be my friend, Alice Rose thought.

"Why, Precious?"

"I'm not sure. I don't know. You're free. You're your own boss. I'm happy you came to Bible class, but then another part of me is kind of disappointed."

"How's that?" Alice Rose asked. She wondered if it was sort of like her half wanting to find the little Chinese boy and half wanting not to.

"You don't exactly fit in, you know."

Alice Rose nodded.

Precious continued, "I like to think that you came to Bible class maybe to be my friend, a true friend!"

Now Alice Rose flushed a deep crimson. This was so embarrassing. True friend! Here she was, star pupil of the world's greatest liar. She had come to Bible class only to spy on the Pettys. And now Precious Petty, with her stupid sausage curls tucked under a rabbit-fur hood, was saying she wanted to be her friend.

"I don't know what you mean by 'true friend,' Precious. I'm just this half-orphan kid. I don't think that your aunt would want me around at all if she didn't think she could save my soul, educate me in the ways of good Christians."

"I know." Precious said the words so quietly, so matter-of-factly, that they caught Alice Rose off guard.

"You know that?" Alice Rose asked.

"Yes, I'm sure you're right. And if she succeeds, I'll probably like you less because then you won't be so . . . so . . ." Precious groped around for a word. "Well, you'll fit in with the rest of us then." Alice Rose had always wanted to fit in, but now she was beginning to see the benefits of *not* fitting in. Maybe, Alice Rose thought, she was a freak like Sam Clemens—one of those unaccountable freaks of nature. She kind of liked that idea.

"Precious, I'm no friend for you. You know my father, he's nice as can be, but he drinks a little and doesn't care what I do. I mean, he lets me stay up all night if I want. He let me quit school. I mean he loves me and all, but . . ."

"And he doesn't make you take too many baths. You've always got dirt behind your ears, Alice Rose."

Alice Rose reddened, then touched her ears. "Yeah, so why do you want to be my friend, Precious? I'm unwashed and unchristian."

"And you swear, too."

"Not often. But why, Precious?"

"I don't know. Some things you just can't explain." Precious sighed. Her cheeks, already pink from the cold, now flared scarlet. She ripped off her furry rabbit hat and stomped it in the snow. "I want to be free, Alice Rose. I want to be free! I hate looking like someone's precious little doll. I hate these curls and these stupid petticoats. I want to wear a duster like you and stomp around in big boots or those high deerskin moccasins you were wearing the other day. I want to be rank and low-down, dirty and unwashed and unchristian and call all the hurdy-gurdy girls by their first names. I hate doing cross-stitched samplers with Bible verses. I want to learn how to turn a ruffle like you did on Juliet Brown's dress over at the Sazerac, or make a flounce like you did for Detta."

Alice Rose stood in the snow with her mouth hanging open. She could hardly believe the torrent of words pouring out of Precious. "But most of all, I hate living with Aunt Jewel and Uncle Horace."

"Well, how come you're living with them and not your parents?"

"My mother ran off."

Alice Rose's eyes sprung open. "Not with a man named Mutch?"

"No. Pierre, a fancy French duke. He has a castle. She's supposed to send for me, but she never does. And my father's so hopping mad about my mother that he's gone plumb crazy. He tried to kill them both, that's why they had to get away. He said he would never let my mother take me off to France. That he would keep me forever. But he kept me for about a month and then decided it was best that I come live with Aunt Jewel and Uncle Horace. And I hate it."

Alice Rose felt terrible for Precious. This was worse than being a half orphan: a mother who was alive but in another country with a man she must love more than Precious, and a father who was half crazy and sent her to live with an aunt and uncle she couldn't stand. All of a sudden, the absolute queerness of Precious's name struck her. Precious was, in fact, precious to no one—at least no one who counted, for Alice Rose did not count Jewel Petty and her husband. No matter how much Precious wanted to be her friend and no matter how much she hated her own aunt and uncle, the fact of life was that grown-ups ran the world. Alice Rose was tempted to tell her why she was really coming to Bible class, but if adults suspected Precious knew something about Alice Rose, they could get it out of her. Alice Rose and Sam's investigation would then be wrecked.

"Look, Precious, I can't take you with me to Chinatown."

"Is this more business of some sort? You always have such interesting business, Alice Rose."

"Well, sort of, not exactly. You know when you live practically on your own there's a lot to do, to take care of." Precious's eyes glistened with a rapturous admiration. "But I'll tell you what."

"What!" Precious nearly jumped out of her rabbit skins.

"How about I let you work on Pie Eye's dress with me. There's going to be lots of ruffles."

"Pie Eye? Who's Pie Eye?"

"Oh, you know, she's that hurdy-gurdy girl over at the Bucket of Blood. She's got one funny eye, but she's nice as can be. She's a good dancer. I figure if I make her huge

sleeves with stand-up ruffles on the shoulders, it might
draw the attention away from her eyes."

"You'd let me help? You really would?"

Good lord, she was so easy to please it almost made
Alice Rose cry. "Of course I would, and you know Buffalo
Jo? Huge gal over at the Flush Times. She weighs over two
hundred and is about as big around as a Conestoga
wagon. Well I'm working on a dress for her now, and I'm
figuring I got a tenth of a mile of ruffles for her dress,
'cause she wants the whole skirt tiered in them. Oh,
you'll learn ruffles all right, Precious. You'll wish you'd
never heard the word."

"No, I won't, Alice Rose. No, I won't." She hurled her
furry body at Alice Rose and embraced her. Alice Rose
felt as if she were being smothered by a stampede of
snowshoe rabbits.

"Hey, look!" Alice Rose shouted. In the distance against
the black and starry night, she saw a plume of snow
swirling up. "It's the Special Express rider."

"What's that?"

"After they shut down the Pony Express, they kept a
few riders on for short hauls to Carson City and Genoa.

If there's something really urgent they'll send it by special. Come on." Alice Rose yanked Precious's hand, and the two girls started running down Sutton. The street was steep, but thick with snow, so they more or less plowed down it in a galumphing gait. Precious was hopeless in her high-button shoes and fell into a deep drift. Alice Rose went back, and though tempted to pull her out by the sausage curls, grabbed her under her arms.

"Sweet Jesus! Precious, you're slower than a snail on crutches. Take your hands out of that darn muff so you can have some balance."

Precious looked up at Alice Rose once more with rapture.

"You swore, Alice Rose!"

"Oh, well, I'm sorry."

"Oh, don't be!"

"Come on, get a move on it or we'll miss him."

The girls stood in the night shadows, just beyond the pool of yellow light cast by the kerosene lamps that hung outside the post office. Raz Clapp had just ridden up and dismounted. "Got a triple star for Judge Petty." He handed the mochilla, a special saddlebag, to Hermie, the postmaster.

"Judge Petty!" Precious exclaimed.

"Triple star means very urgent. You could take it right to him."

"No, I couldn't. Aunt and Uncle would have a fit if they knew I was down here." Precious's eyes never left the rider and the sweating pony whose panting made the still night throb with an intense rhythm. Raz Clapp was breathing heavily, too, as they led a fresh pony out from behind the post office.

"The riders have to be young and lightweight. If you and I were boys we could be Special Express riders. Wouldn't that be the beatingest!" Alice Rose whispered.

Hermie handed Raz a steaming mug of coffee. He took a couple of swallows, then leaped on the fresh pony, whirled it around, and was off in a swirl of snow. The girls watched him as far as they could, until the swirl of snow was swept up by the night and dissolved into the black nothingness of the dark valley below.

The girls said good night, and Precious headed back up

Sutton Street and Alice Rose down toward E Street. She wondered what Judge Petty's important message was. Triple-Star letters sent by Special Express cost upward of twenty dollars!

Chapter 17

IT WAS AMAZING how quickly the people of Chinatown had begun rebuilding. The Cave of the Dragon Sleepers was back in business. Actually, it was hard to burn down a place that was dug into a hillside and walled with rough rocks. The pale yellow light seeped out from behind the small door. There was not a sound. This was one of the main differences between an opium den and a saloon. The dens were enveloped in a deathly stillness. She knew that she would not find Hop Sing there. Hop Sing hated anything to do with opium. She might find him in one of the gambling dens, although he watched more than he ever gambled.

She approached a shack strung together out of paper and scrap wood. She walked up to the door and peeked through a crack. A dozen or more men were huddled on the earthen benches carved out of the side of the hill. In the dim pool of light, she could see dice flying through the air and hitting the ground with a soft *plink*. Although her view was limited, she could see no sign of Hop Sing. So she continued through the five densely packed blocks of Chinatown to the most western end, where Hop Sing and his distant cousin from Shanghai had built themselves one of the more substantial shacks in Chinatown. Their main construction material for the frame was discarded wagon wheels. They had sheathed this in scraps of tar paper and tin. Alice Rose knocked lightly on the door. A voice sang out. The words sounded like *aht cha!*

"It's me, Alice Rose."

"Alice Rose!"

The door scraped open. Hop Sing stood before her, a long pipe in his mouth, wearing a long quilted coat and his little box hat. "What you doing here? Out on cold night like this. Come in. I fix you some good black tea." Within two minutes, Hop Sing had fixed her a bowl of tea, which she held in her hands for warmth. "You need something to eat." This was always an adventure

that was seldom pleasing as far as Alice Rose was concerned, except of course when there were noodles.
From the coals of the fire in the tin drum, which func-
tioned as a stove, he poked at something with a long
forked stick. Grabbing it between the prongs, he
dragged it from the coals. "Ah, perfect!" he whispered as
he slid it onto a tin plate. Charred and lumpy, it was too
small to be a potato but about the right size for a wild
goat turd. Alice Rose's stomach turned. "What is it?"

"You see." Hop Sing got out a glittering knife with a
paper-thin blade and deftly sliced the lump. Steam
poured from it. "Chian Fong Shang."

"Huh?"

"Ah, hard to translate. In Shanghai Province means
Delight of the Thousand Phoenix Rising."

This did not explain a lot to Alice Rose. "Is there a bird
in there?"

"Ah no. No meat." For some reason, this relieved Alice
Rose until she tried the first bite. It tasted like dirt, dirt
mixed with tar. "Just bean—bean paste wrapped in
dough." How could a bean taste this bad, she wondered.
Thousand Phoenix Rising, my foot! thought Alice Rose as

she tried to swallow the heavy, sticky bite. This thing couldn't have gotten two inches off the ground! I'd have a better chance of flying than this bean turd.

"You need some soy sauce?" Hop Sing asked.

"Maybe." Alice Rose tried her best not to make a face and she hoped, since she wasn't so good with chopsticks, that some of the dumpling might fall on the floor. She took another bite. The soy sauce helped.

"So why you here, Alice Rose? Little boy again with mummy wrapped in yellow silk."

Alice Rose nodded.

"I ask all over Chinatown. No one knows what boy you are talking about. They say maybe Bing Fong's son, but then someone remember that Bing Fong's son went back to San Francisco before fire."

"Who started the fire, Hop Sing? What about the thing that was written on the sign at the Cave of the Dragon Sleepers?"

Hop Sing made a face, waved his hand in contempt.

"You don't believe that?" Alice Rose asked.

"Oh, I believe it was started, all right. I just don't believe that sign at Dragon Sleepers. First of all, opium dens don't have signs. Everyone in Chinatown know that. So someone made that sign with dragon and wrote on it."

"What did they write?"

"I don't know. Something from your holy book."

"It wasn't something about the young lion and the dragon shalt thou trample under feet, was it?"

"I don't know. Doesn't matter."

"Doesn't matter! Hop Sing, they nearly burned all of Chinatown down. A lot of people died."

"I know that, Alice Rose. I'm not dumb, but all this stuff about the Christian people doing it because of opium dens is silly. That was not why they burned us down. That was an excuse."

"Excuse for what, Hop Sing?"

Hop Sing dragged the bucket he was sitting on closer and leaned toward Alice Rose. His almond eyes dark and reflecting nothing; his face brown as a nut with fine lines fanning out across his cheeks. It was impossible to tell how old Hop Sing was. He might be forty or he might be seventy. "Alice Rose, white folks here like us smoking opium and not owning feet in the Comstock. They like to keep us dumb; that's why they have laws to keep us from

going to school. They care if Chinese don't buy opium
with their dollars; they care if the Chinese heads get clear
of opium smoke, wake up, and decide to buy mines and
land instead, especially now that Confederacy is broke.
Others get smart, too. They know feet in Comstock do
them better than opium in pipe. But hard to buy because
laws say Chinamen can't own land. Some brokers don't
care if Chinese buy. They just charge a big commission.
Word starts to get around, however. Gossip again. People
hear that Chinese are buying feet in Comstock Lode."

Alice Rose scratched her head and thought about what
Hop Sing had just told her.

"Alice Rose, it's late. It's Christmas Eve, you should be
home with your papa."

Of course, that was why they were having the Bible
class tonight with the special cider, cake, and cookies, and
why her father had said he'd be home early. Christmas
Eve! Good lord, she had clean forgotten.

Chapter 18

DESPITE THE FREEZING TEMPERATURES, by the time Alice Rose raced up the stairs and into the apartment, she was sweating.

"Dad! Dad! I'm sorry." She paused. "Oh, no!" she moaned. There was her father snoring softly in his easy chair. A bit of Christmas ribbon was draped over one ear. There was a half-empty glass of whiskey beside him, and three pretty packages on the kitchen table. She tiptoed in and got the gifts she had made for her father and put them beside the presents on the table.

"Oh, Alice Rose!" Her father sat up in the chair, scratching his head. The ribbon around his ear fell off, and he gave a brief snort. "We were celebrating over at the Sazerac, but I came home and no Alice Rose! Where you been, honey?"

"Well, I was over at Jewel Petty's Bible class, and then I went down to see Hop Sing, and oh, Dad, I feel terrible. I just clean forgot it was Christmas Eve."

Stanley Tucker looked at his daughter and smiled sweetly. "Oh, Alice Rose, don't you go feeling bad."

"But the one night you came home early on purpose."

"Well, A. R., think of all those other nights when I don't do anything on purpose and stay out late just foolin' around with the boys." There was an unusual note in her father's voice, a tinge of regret more than melancholy.

"Dad, you all right?"

"I'm fine. Now don't you go worrying about me."

"Do you miss Mother?"

"Of course, not a day goes by I don't miss her, and tonight I missed you."

"Oh, Dad!" Alice Rose ran over to where her father sat and fell to her knees, burying her head in his lap.

"Don't cry, Alice Rose! Don't cry."

"But you missed me and it was all my fault."

"But on all the other nights it was my fault. And you know Alice Rose, sometimes missing someone is a good thing. It reminds you of how special someone really is."

Alice Rose lifted her head and blinked away the tears. "Yes, I'm saying you are special, dear child. And I know if I were in my right mind, I would send you back to live with Aunt Eugenia. This is no proper place for a child. But to tell you the truth, Alice Rose, right now I think I would just miss you too darned much. Aside from that, I really couldn't afford to send you back. But if some of these feet over in the Yellow Jacket mine in Gold Hill start paying off, well maybe by this time next year." Alice Rose could hardly believe her ears. This was the best Christmas present ever. "Now that you're back, let's start the celebration. You know you missed Sam Clemens. He brought a present over specially for you. They're all on the table there. Mr. Clemens's, mine, and a rather large box from Aunt Eugenia."

"And I got yours, Dad."

"Well, let's start. There's some hot cocoa on the stove. And let's see, I think there is a bottle of peppermint schnapps in the cupboard. That will be my libation of choice, if you will fetch it."

Alice Rose poured her cocoa and her father's schnapps.

They began with Aunt Eugenia's presents. In the big box there were several presents for both her and her father. A pouch of very fine Leavitt and Pearce tobacco from Uncle Wiley's favorite tobacconist over in Cambridge, near Harvard College; also for her father a thick knitted vest that Aunt Eugenia had made. But Alice Rose's gifts were the most wonderful: a cashmere shawl in a soft pink color, a lovely nightgown with fretwork, and best of all, two volumes of poetry and a book of drawings of Italian monuments. Next she opened her father's present. It was big, but light. She unwrapped layer upon layer of tissue paper. "Oh!" gasped Alice Rose. Nestled in the sheets of tissue paper were a pair of knee-high, pure-white buck-skin winter moccasins with beautiful turquoise beading, and beside them a buff-colored pouch, also beaded. "Oh, Dad, you must have paid a fortune for these."

"Well, let's put it this way: there's one Paiute squaw out there a heck of a lot richer tonight."

"Is it Winnemucca's daughter Mary? It looks like her beadwork."

"Yes. I only go to the best."

She threw her arms around her father. "Oh, Dad! You

know how I just love moccasins. They're so comfortable, and my old pair are about shot!"

"Yes, well just you remember. You can wear moccasins here in Virginia City, but back in Boston folks are bound to look mighty queer at you."

"You're right about that. Now it's time for you to open your present."

He unwrapped the package and held up a pair of hand-knit socks. "Ah, Alice Rose! You are so clever. Won't I be the envy of the boys."

"And I knitted them double thick because I know how cold your feet get, Dad."

"Well, you better open Sam's gift to you, A. R."

It was a heavy package. She unwrapped it. It was a book, *The Count of Monte Cristo.* It was not brand-new, but rather worn with age. The cloth cover was frayed at the edges, and a dark stain dimmed the gold gilt of part of the title. She opened it up. A note fell out.

Dear Alice Rose,
This book is about treasure which I know is the last thing you care hearing about living right smack on top the biggest silver bonanza of the world.

Nonetheless, it is a good yarn, and I read it over and over again when I was a youngster growing up on the river. There is even a little bit of the river in this book—literally; for you will notice many of the pages, including the cover, are stained with the waters of the Mississippi. I used to like to take it to read down on the banks, or when my friend Tom Blankenship and I would "borrow a skiff" or make ourselves a raft to float downriver a piece. Sometimes all you need in life is a good yarn, and you're blessed if it can be enjoyed on a great river. So there is in a way a little of both in this water-stained book for you. Merry Christmas, Alice Rose. You have been a true friend.

Sincerely,
Samuel Clemens

Chapter 19

BINGE. ALICE ROSE WROTE the word down on her hate list. She supposed she was going to have to get around to alphabetizing the list one of these days, because here was *Binge* coming after *Depth* and *Down.* But *Binge* with a capital *B* was exactly what her father, Sam Clemens, Dan De Quille, and the whole lot of the boys from the *Enterprise* had been on for the last four days, since Artemus Ward the famous humorist writer and speaker had come to town to give a series of lectures at the Maguire Opera House.

It seemed to Alice Rose that the warm glow of the Christmas Eve she and her father had shared had hardly lasted through the next day. Ward had arrived on Christmas, and they had gone to see his show. He was funny. Alice Rose gave him that. He would stand up there and mangle words and speak seeming nonsense and generally fool around. But the fooling around continued offstage. Ward had found true brothers with the lot at the *Enterprise*. He took to sleeping there, which only amounted to brief periods between bouts of carousing through the town. Last night they had all gone down to Chinatown, not to the opium dens but to the brandy parlors.

The "Companions of the Jug" as they called themselves had spent the wee hours of the morning at a brewery that conveniently backed up to the *Enterprise* offices. The beer was a dollar a gallon and it came, for an extra twenty-five cents, with Limburger cheese, radishes, mustard, and caraway. As far as Alice Rose could see, that is all that they ate during the four-day binge. If the binge had started any other day but Christmas, that day would not have tarnished so quickly and lost its glow. She nearly put it on her hate list. But then she decided that Christmas was not the problem. Christmas was good; it was binges that were bad.

Alice Rose now sat stitching by the window. Precious would be here soon. She had the strips for the ruffles of Pie Eye's dress cut and had shown Precious yesterday how to make the parallel lines of basting stitches so they could be gathered in just the right way. Precious had learned fairly quickly.

It was almost time for her to go to the *Enterprise*. She had promised Steve Gillis that she would help him set up type trays. The other boys were supposed to be writing. There was a lot of mining news. Several rich strikes had started before Christmas and now there was a speculation frenzy erupting. Out of the Ophir, Gould, Curry, and Mexican mines on the Comstock lead, huge carloads of silver-rich ore were being brought up each day.

Alice Rose put down her needle and thread, wrote a note to Precious with instructions about what was to be stitched, and said she would be back in an hour. She bundled herself into a long-tailed winter coat of her father's which she had cut down for herself, and slipped into her new moccasins. From a hook she took a wide-brimmed fur-lined leather buffalo-hunter's hat that she had found in the dump. It kept her ears warm and was as good as an umbrella against the falling snow. Shielded against the bitter cold, she set out for the *Enterprise* offices, wending her way through the quartz wagons that carried the raw rock to the crushing mills. The streets were foggy with the breath of the hauling animals. Donkey, burrow, ox, and horse strained with their rich loads, while expelling small clouds through their frosty muzzles.

The boys liked to sit around a long table to write their stories, and this morning they were sitting there dutifully writing, except for two. Stretched out sound asleep in the middle of the table was Artemus Ward. Ophira, the office cat, strolled casually over his belly. Ambling around the table, in a cloud of foul-smelling smoke from the pipe that his companions called the Remains, was Sam Clemens. He was holding forth on how this was a newspaper office and not a hotel, but that perhaps they should turn it into one.

"If I ran a hotel," the Missouri drawl curled lazily out of the smoke cloud, "here would be the rules: this house is strictly intemperate. None but the brave deserve the fare." There were guffaws at this, although Alice Rose did notice that her father seemed to be concentrating on his proofreading. "Boarders who do not wish to pay in advance are requested to advance and pay."

"Hah!" The laughter broke out full now, and Stanley

Tucker put down his blue pencil. Even Alice Rose chuckled slightly. "Persons owing bills for board will be bored for bill. Double boarders can have two beds with a room in it, or two rooms with a bed in it, as they choose. Single men and their families will not be boarded. Dreams will be charged for by the dozen."

Artemus Ward began to stir. "Can't a man get a decent night's sleep around here?" he asked, rising to a sitting position on the table. "What's that child doing in here?" They all turned to look at Alice Rose.

"The child," she spoke precisely, "is here to see if Steve Gillis needs any help today doing what you're all supposed to be doing—getting out a newspaper—but can't because half the time you've been out on the town carousing."

"Thanks, Alice Rose," Steve Gillis said, standing up from the table, "but I think we're getting into pretty good shape here. Everybody's got their stories in and been generally behaving themselves."

"You don't say," she replied. Alice Rose had not had occasion to meet with Sam Clemens about the Bible classes or to discuss any of the new developments, such as Hop Sing's information about Chinese buying feet in Comstock Lode and how this worried white folks, especially Confederate white folks. She would not tell him that she had become Hop Sing's partner. She wasn't sure what Mr. Clemens would think of that. Better to be quiet about it.

This seemed like a good time. Except for Sam Clemens, who was reloading the Remains with fresh tobacco, the boys had gone back to their writing.

"Mr. Clemens," Alice Rose said in a low voice. "We need to talk."

"You got a new story for me?"

"No, the same old one with some new twists."

"Well, why don't we adjourn to the brewery, it being so close."

"Why not the Sazerac, it being so much cleaner and not smelling of beer and Limburger cheese."

"Fine. I'm not picky at this hour of the morning."

"What'll it be, Alice Rose?" Sam Clemens asked as the bartender came up. Ben Warren was nowhere in sight.

"Coffee with half milk."

"And for me, molasses with a touch of gin."

Alice Rose wrinkled her nose in disgust.

"On your tab, Mark?" the bartender asked.

Alice Rose looked around to see who the bartender was talking to.

"Mark Twain," Sam Clemens replied.

"I thought you told me that was a river call." Alice Rose said.

"It is. It means two fathoms, safe water."

"Well, how come you're using it here?" she asked.

"I don't know, means two. Nice way of saying mark down two drinks. Got a ring to it."

"It does," Alice Rose said reflectively. "Is that why Eddie called you Mark?"

"Yes, seems like all the bartenders 'round town know me more as Mark than Sam."

"You ever thought of having a pen name?" Alice Rose asked. "Artemus Ward's real name is Charles Browne. You could have one, too. With all those lies you write it might come in handy."

"Yes, it might."

The coffee and the gin with molasses came. Alice Rose

told Sam Clemens about the Chinese buying feet in the Comstock, but not about her partnership in the mining claim with Hop Sing. "I was about to quit Bible class, but I don't know. Precious actually isn't so bad. She thinks I'm her best friend."

"Are you?"

"Well, she thinks I am. I don't mind being her friend. I guess if you think someone is your best friend, they are. I mean from her point of view, I am her best friend, the person she most wants to be friends with. I'm not sure if she is my best friend." Alice Rose thought, how could she be, when in fact she was hiding so much from Precious? She had come to Bible class under false pretenses. You didn't do that to best friends. She bit her lip lightly and thought. "Mr. Clemens, I got to tell you something."

"What's that, Alice Rose?"

"Mr. Clemens, I left out a part about the Chinese buying feet?"

"What part would that be?"

"The fact is, Mr. Clemens, I filled out a claim in my name for Hop Sing. We became partners on some feet up at the top of the Ophir. It was bought with money Hop

Sing had. I just basically did the paperwork and let him use my name. Hop Sing feels real strong about Chinese not spending money for opium. He hates opium. He wants land, feet, rights in mines, but you know the laws."

Sam Clemens nodded. His face was quite grave. "This seems like something you should be telling your father. Why are you telling me this, Alice Rose?"

"I guess because you're my best friend." Alice Rose looked down at her hands. She could feel the color rising in her cheeks. There was a pause that seemed to last forever and a day. She could hear a wild wind beginning to raise a ruckus outside.

"Well, guess what Alice Rose?"

"What?"

"I reckon you're my best friend, too, out here."

"You mean that, Mr. Clemens?"

"Of course I mean it. For Lord's sake, you brought me my first story. Not to mention countless other things for local items."

"Oh, local items," scoffed Alice Rose. "Those don't count." Local items were the small news items, generally of a noncriminal nature that most often had little to do with mining or silver strikes.

"They certainly do count. We have to get at least twelve inches a day out of local items. I've gotten eight inches out of thumbless boys alone. I'm working on one now."

"Somebody new blow off their thumb?" Alice Rose asked.

"No, I'm waiting for the first girl, though."

"So what's this story you're working on?"

"Oh, it's an utterly charming piece. I mean piece literally here."

"What?"

"I'm interviewing a thumb."

"What?"

"Yes, a thumb of a certain Benny Schmitt that was found in some sagebrush just outside the schoolhouse window. Blown-off thumbs make marvelous interviews."

"Good Lord, Mr. Clemens." Alice Rose rested her chin in her hand and looked at the wild man next to her. "What will you think of next? You really better start using another name. What are Benny's parents going to think?"

"Well, they might be upset that the thumb has no interest whatsoever in reuniting with Benny."

"Why's that?" It was impossible not to be drawn into these bizarre conversations with Sam Clemens.

"Well, according to the thumb, Benny always blamed his poor penmanship on him—the thumb. The thumb claims that the kid didn't have any more sense than a boiled carrot and did not know how to properly hold a writing instrument." Sam Clemens set down his drink. "In any case, enough of the thumb. Tomorrow I have to go over to Carson City to start covering the second Territorial Legislature. Again I shall look into this thing concerning Mutch running off with the preacher's wife, but I don't have high hopes. I think we're chasing a red herring with this."

"But why would someone hire some fancy dude to come down and shoot an old drunk like Mutch?"

"I don't know. But I think what is more important is the Chinatown fire and the Society of Seven connection. You've turned up a good piece with the information Hop Sing gave you about the Chinese buying feet. Again, a deliberate mislead, the writing scrawled on the sign of the Cave of the Dragon Sleepers, red herring. Hop Sing's right. They don't give a hoot about opium. It's the Chinamen having a stake in the Comstock that's got them worried. Think about this: the Society of Seven is mixed up with the Confederacy. The Confederacy is nearly bankrupt. They need that silver."

"You think I should keep going to Bible class?"

"Alice Rose, I've got a hunch something is bound to turn up sooner or later. There is a nasty plot afoot here. This town is ripe for it. It doesn't know what side of the darned war it wants to be on. We've got Confederates and Union people holding the Comstock hostage. Their best foot into that is through Eilley Orrum's central lead. This man Willy Carter, he's the meanest son of a gun I've ever come across, loaded to the muzzle with rage. You got to be patient in this newspaper business, Alice Rose."

"All right. I'll keep going. But how long are you going to be gone for?"

"Two, three weeks. I'll be back some time in between. You can always send a message to me. The *Enterprise* has got a pouch going back and forth on the stage every day during the legislature for the dispatches."

They got up to walk outside, and as they stepped through the door an enormous zephyr slammed down C Street. Suddenly, Alice Rose felt herself whipped up and thrown into the air. She sailed off the boardwalk and halfway across the street, until she smacked into something rough and broad.

"Alice Rose!" Ben Warren exclaimed, peeling her off his chest. "Good lord, child, we better put a sea anchor on you." He set her down on the ground and bending over he patted her shoulders. She was caught in the fierce blue light of his eyes. His lean hawkish face was close to hers. His thick mustache was frosted. This is simply too much, flying and being one inch away from Ben Warren's face, Alice Rose thought. I'm going to have some romantic affliction like those ladies in the novels that mother read to me. I'm going to need smelling salts and all there is in this fool town is a steaming pile of mule poop. And Alice Rose was standing right in it in her lovely new white buckskin moccasins.

"Oh, jeez, Alice Rose look what I've done to you." Ben Warren gasped. "I didn't mean to set you down there."

"My new Christmas moccasins!"

"Don't worry!"

Before she knew it he had picked her up again and was carrying her back into the Sazerac. If she could have forgotten the mule poop on her moccasins, it would have seemed romantic.

For the next twenty minutes Alice Rose felt as if she was in some sort of weird dream world. There was Ben Warren gently unlacing her moccasins. "Don't worry I have a remedy for this. It's foolproof. It's hundred proof!" He laughed as he took a bottle of clear liquid from under the counter. "Potato juice with alcohol. More commonly know as vodka. No smell."

"I wish it did. I don't want to smell like manure every time I put on my moccasins."

Within fifteen minutes, Ben Warren had the moccasins restored to their former pristine beauty. There was not one speck of mule manure. The soft buckskin glistened white.

"See, it's like a miracle!" he said.

Alice Rose nodded silently. She felt as if she were in a trance. The whole thing was like a miracle. She wouldn't mind getting picked up by a Washoe zephyr every day of the week and being drenched in mule poop if it meant . . . oh dear, she was falling in love!

"How's my dress coming?" It was Carla who interrupted her reverie.

"Oh, fine, Carla. I got it all cut out. You'll have to come over in a few days for a fitting." Alice Rose felt as if someone else was speaking. She laced up her moccasins and left.

It was only when she was a block away that she remembered that she had forgotten to thank Mr. Warren for cleaning up her moccasins. It was then she came to her senses. Thank Ben Warren for setting me down in a pile of mule poop? I must be out of my mind! If this is what love does, I want no part of it. With a determined step and watchful of where the mules had trod, Alice Rose made her way home.

Chapter 20

At sunset yesterday, the wind commenced blowing
after a fashion to which a typhoon is mere nonsense,
and in a short time, the face of heaven was obscured
by vast clouds of dust and spangled over with lum-
ber and shingles and dogs and things, including one
medium-sized child, a girl, who was picked up by
the aforementioned wind and slammed into the proprietor of the Sazerac saloon.

This was Alice Rose's first mention in print. She had
clipped the article from the *Enterprise* and was pasting it
in a book she had started to keep of Sam Clemens arti-
cles. But now Alice Rose picked up the paper with a column that had just been printed today, a dispatch from

Carson City dated January 31, 1863. It was a column about a party Sam Clemens had attended. She began to reread it and got to her favorite part. Precious was hemming up a dress. "Listen to this, Precious. This is what is so funny about Mr. Clemens. Here he writes about this fancy mansion where the party was. He says the walls are 'garnished with pictures and above all, mirrors, wherein you may gaze, and always find something to admire, you know.'" Alice Rose giggled at this. Precious just kept on sewing. Didn't Precious think that was funny? She guessed she just didn't get it. It got funnier. Maybe Precious would get the next part. "'I have a great regard for a good house, and a girlish passion for mirrors.'"

"But he's a man, Alice Rose," Precious said.

"That's the point, Precious. That's why it's so darned funny."

Alice Rose sighed. She had taught Precious how to sew and taught her how to swear, but she guessed you just plain couldn't teach a person how to laugh. She got the scissors and clipped the article. The other reason the dispatch from Carson City was special for Alice Rose was that instead of his usual byline of S. Clemens, he had signed this one Mark Twain. He had indeed taken Alice Rose's advice.

Winter began to slip into spring. The shadow of Mount Davidson retreated a bit each week, until light washed down the steep slopes and into the town from morning to midafternoon. The streets turned to mud and Sam Clemens returned from Carson City. The case against Eilley Orrum was getting set to be tried. Alice Rose continued with Bible class so dutifully that Jewel Petty could not contain her enthusiasm about her newest convert, the "half-orphan" she had snatched from spiritual oblivion. Word got back to Alice Rose that Jewel Petty had been bragging about her rescue of this "poor lost girl" whom she had brought into the bosom of Christianity. Alice Rose thought she'd throw up. But she just figured it was all in the line of business, and sooner or later, it would pay off. Then she would really cut loose and Jewel Petty could just rot.

Come March, Sam Clemens insisted on renting two old plugs and taking her out into the high desert country to see what he called "desert bloom."

"You look down into the throat of that cactus blossom, Alice Rose, and you tell me if you have ever seen anything prettier."

They were on a high desert plain, several miles out of Virginia City. The wind was still cold. She wore her buffalo hat and duster with layers of sweaters underneath. The air was dry and crisp, the sky a startling blue. The landscape was a dull dun color, but every few feet some extraordinary blossom popped out of the thorniest, ugliest cactus. The color of the blossom, the very shape was arresting in its vivid beauty.

She now peered down the throat of the cactus blossom. It looked like a dark scarlet heaven bursting with constellations. The early morning dew bathed every blossom in a trembling radiance. Within one dewdrop, the sky, the clouds, and the sun were reflected. Alice Rose sat with Sam Clemens and watched the dew evaporate in the warming day. She watched the reflection of sky and clouds be quenched by the sun, only to be born again on another desert morning.

Mr. Clemens never knew the name of a plant, but he seemed to have a familiarity with them nonetheless. "You strip the leaves off that thing and it makes a very fine tea, supposedly cures the scours if you are so afflicted." When she pressed him about names of plants and what they could do, he got edgy. Finally he burst out, "Alice Rose, it's just plain not good to know everything about everything."

"How can you say that? You're a reporter, a journalist. We're trying to find out everything about Mutch and his murderer and the cursed Society of Seven and what we know they did in Chinatown. It *is* important to know everything about everything."

"No, Alice Rose, not if you really love it. Not a thing of beauty!" Alice Rose felt completely lost. What was he talking about?

He began to walk toward her. He carried in his hand a delicate trumpet-shaped blossom that had blown off a cactus. He twirled it between his fingers. "Alice Rose, I once told you that to know God is to know nature, that I knew a river once and that was as close as I ever came to knowing God."

Alice Rose nodded.

"I learned that river by heart. I carried the shape of that

river in my head and knew every point, bend, bar, island, and reach. I kept a notebook and wrote down page after page of notes. I learned how to recognize the meaning of every wrinkle and curl of the water. A silver streak meant a new snag, a slick meant dangerous shoaling, and dimpled water marked a sunken wreck. I learned how to shave an island so close as to brush the deckhouse with the overhanging branches. Oh yes, I learned that river. It was like a wonderful, fascinating book. But as I learned to read the book I found that the poetry of the river was lost. I came to value its features for their usefulness rather than for their beauty. I quit before I lost the rapture. I did not want to lose my God."

As they walked back to their horses that day, Alice Rose stopped abruptly. On a large, smooth, flat rock a desert snail made its way. The sun caught a glistening trail.

"Whatcha lookin' at, Alice Rose?"

"This snail. See that glistening trail. It starts over there at the edge of the rock. Does it signify anything to you?"

"Signifies that it's a confused snail that doesn't know where it wants to go?"

"You read any letters in that?" Alice Rose asked.

Sam Clemens crouched close to the ground. "I don't know. Maybe an *L*, could be an *O*." He pointed. "And a *W* possibly."

"I thought it looked more like an *M*, but I suppose it depends on which direction you view it from. Oh well, let's go." Alice Rose never found another snail and didn't give that one any thought until many years later.

Spring slid imperceptibly into summer. Alice Rose kept going to Bible class. She was learning a lot about the Bible, but that was about all. Jewel Petty not only read the Bible but knew every bend and turn and, as Alice Rose was beginning to understand, was blind to the snags. For Jewel Petty, God was not wonderful at all. He was not mysterious. He looked exactly like her—fat, double-chinned, with gold rimmed spectacles that rested on fat little cheeks. The only difference was that He was a man.

Chapter 21

"It could have been some celebration, had we only known!" Eilley Orrum said as she admired herself in the mirror in another new dress that Alice Rose had just finished for her.

"Turn." Alice Rose spoke through a mouthful of pins.

"What's this stupid rule, Alice Rose, about the journalistic monopoly?"

Alice Rose wished that Eilley would not ask her all these questions when she had pins in her mouth. Thankfully, Andy Drake spoke up. "It's not such a stupid rule. I thank heaven for it. It merely forbids revealing eastern news before it's published in San Francisco. This town is bad enough on the Fourth of July. If folks had found out Vicksburg had fallen and the Union armies

were victorious at Gettysburg, all hell would have broken
loose. Those Copperheads are going to be meaner than
ever, Eilley, and a lot of that venom is going to come right
down on your head."

"Vein number fifty-two, my central lead." Eilley
Orrum smacked her lips together, her eyes glinting play-
fully. For the life of her, Alice Rose could not understand
Eilley's attitude. Yes, she was irritated, but only slightly.

"Turn," Alice Rose said again.

"Well, to review our strategy, Eilley." Andy Drake
walked back to a table where some papers were spread.
"We cannot underestimate Carter. He will stoop to anything. He is a great seducer of juries. I've seen him work
before. In court, he'll pursue the multiledge theory. Of
course, this sounds quite democratic and every juror will
see that he too could become part owner of the richest
vein in the Comstock. According to this theory, every
dip, angle, and spur that comes within fifty feet of the
main vein could claim that vein for its grandpappy."

"Grand*mammy*," Eilley said. "Don't you think you
should nip that in a bit more where the bodice meets the
flounce, Alice Rose?"

"Grandmammy," Andy Drake repeated. "We, of course, favor the single ledge theory. We can trace this single ledge of the central vein number fifty-two as running completely through the Comstock, and you hold all the claims that run every single foot of the way just about to the very top."

Alice Rose wondered if anyone owned the top.

The talk went on and on, Alice Rose only half listening. Andy Drake finally bade them farewell. The trial was set to begin within two weeks.

Eilley took a few more turns in front of the mirror. "Alice Rose, tell you what. If I have any money left after this whole thing is over, I'm going to take you to Paris with me and show you off to Musheur Gagelin. He won't believe his eyes."

"And if you don't?" Alice Rose asked.

"Don't what?"

"Don't have any money left. What will you do without your money?"

"Oh, Alice Rose!" Eilley bent over and took Alice Rose's hand between hers. "Come over here and sit down a spell. Let me talk to you. I don't have any pins anyplace that's going to make me squawk when I sit, do I?"

"No."

"Now you listen to me, Alice Rose Tucker. Everybody's got their bloomers in a bunch worrying about me losing my money. Now I can't claim that it'll be the best thing that ever happened, and I certainly hate the thought of those Copperhead Confederates latching on to it. But you know all of this—" She waved her hand at the plaster moldings with the clusters of grapes, the crystal chandeliers, and the rich oriental carpets. "All this isn't worth a hill of beans if I can't be free. And I am free with this stuff or without it, rich as Croesus or poor as a church mouse. If I went broke tomorrow and had to go back to my cabin over in Johnson City and cook pork and beans for miners, it wouldn't be the worst thing that ever happened to me. No, the worst thing that ever happened to me is when I lost my two babies. One lived just a month, the other four months. The second worst thing that ever happened to me was when I took it into my head to read those initials wrong. Read them as E. H. instead of S. B. and wound up as number-four wife of that fool Mormon. But this is just money, Alice Rose. Just money. I shouldn't have to tell you that. You got more sense than half the people in this town. You, of all people, haven't been fooled by the big magnet of the Comstock Lode. You're just like your mother."

Alice Rose pressed her lips together and felt a quaky sensation inside her chest. What Eilley said about money and being free was probably true. But how could you have as much money as Eilley and not worry about losing it? Alice Rose looked at Eilley sitting there in the beautiful blue glacé silk dress with the yellow roses. She pictured her in the rough homespun dress and thick stockings of the frontier women, miners' wives who toiled under the harshest of conditions. Either way, Eilley still looked the same. Dark eyes, straight nose, firm mouth ready to smile. There would be no difference. It suddenly dawned on Alice Rose that Eilley Orrum was the one person in the entire Nevada Territory who could walk away from it all and never look back, not once. That alone made her the most powerful person Alice Rose had ever met.

Eilley gave her hand another pat. "You run along now, dear. One of my carpenters is taking a buckboard up to Virginia City for a load of nails. He'll give you a ride."

"All right, Eilley. You look real pretty in that dress."

"I look real pretty in my common worsted trousers with a skirt thrown over them, knee-deep in snow out in the gulch cooking for a bunch of ornery miners, too." Eilley winked as she walked Alice Rose to the door. But Eilley Orrum, Alice Rose knew, could never be just common, either on the inside or on the outside.

Chapter 22

ON THE WAY BACK, Alice Rose had noticed there were scatters of pale pink and rose flowers similar to sweet peas along the roadside. She told the driver to let her off a mile or so outside of town. She would walk the rest of the way and gather the flowers, then go to the cemetery. In four days it would be the first anniversary of her mother's and Perry's death. It was, in fact, her birthday, the day her mother did not die on. Alice Rose had turned thirteen. Her father had given her a present, a pretty silk scarf that he had ordered all the way from San Francisco. It was good of him to remember.

She had not been out to the cemetery since the night she met Hop Sing. She didn't have a container for the flowers, but still she would spread them on the graves. As she approached the graves, to her relief she saw that the coyote cheats were there, and no rattlers were in sight. It still made Alice Rose's blood run cold when she remembered the huge rattlesnake that had been sitting atop little Perry's grave that night.

She arranged the blossoms around the coyote cheats. She supposed she could remove the stones entirely. After all, what was left in those coffins now but bones? Nothing to attract a desert predator. She sat down a piece to think. She still missed her mother something awful. People said you got used to the missing, but she didn't think this was really true. She didn't think she would ever get used to it. No, she would get tired of it. Yes, she was already tired of it, tired of missing her mom. It was time for her to come back. Say it was all just a mistake. Then Alice Rose wouldn't have to be alone anymore. She got up to leave. She did not want to think of her mother as bones. She was so much more than that. So much more.

Chapter 23

THE TRIAL HAD STARTED. It was not going well. The jurors, as far as Alice Rose could tell, were mostly "secesh" as the saying went, secessionists. They wanted nothing more than to claim the central lead of the number fifty-two for Jefferson Davis, president of the Confederacy. Judge Petty seemed to be trying to be fair. He sustained many of Andy Drake's objections and twice cautioned Willy Carter that he was bordering on contempt of court and should mind himself.

Sam Clemens and Joe Goodman sat in the area reserved for the press. There were two reporters from the other newspaper in Virginia City, the *Union,* and one from a paper in Carson City. It was an important case.

The courtroom was packed with muttering men from each side, Union and Confederate, each with an opinion, each with a gun.

By the third day of the trial, the judge's evenhandedness was getting to Carter. He had not expected this from a judge he felt had Confederate sympathies. He now rose with deliberation and went to a wall where, with a flourish, he pulled down a map. "It is the intention of the plaintiff, the Rodham Mining Company, in their suit against Eilley Orrum, to introduce incontrovertible evidence of a one-hundred-fifty-foot granite vein, more commonly known as a 'horse' by miners, which lies like an underground fence between the claims of the Rodham Company and the central vein number fifty-two of Eilley Orrum. This horse shall prove beyond all reasonable doubt that there is no such thing as a single continuous ledge, that indeed one must subscribe to the multiledge theory. In addition to presenting this map, I shall call in the afternoon session a number of witnesses who will support the horse claim."

Carter sat down.

"Objection, your honor." Now Andy Drake stood. "No

witnesses not heretofore registered and entered in the court record may be introduced, according to section B article 31, Rules of Jurisprudence in the Territory of Nevada, as passed by the Second Territorial Session in Carson City, November 1862."

"Objection overruled."

Gasps swept across the courtroom. Even the Confederates seemed surprised, but then they burst into cheers. Judge Petty quickly banged the gavel and called for order.

At the noon recess, Sam Clemens pulled Alice Rose aside.

"You still going to Bible class?"

"Yes, of course."

"I sure wish it met every night of the week."

"What are you trying to do, kill me, Mr. Clemens?"

"Something is starting to smell mighty rotten in this courtroom."

Alice Rose had an idea. Jewel Petty knew that Alice Rose had done some sewing around town. Precious had said that her aunt wanted some summer gowns. "Look, Precious's aunt wants me to make some dresses for her. I can tell her that some new fabrics have come in and I can bring them over and say if I could work on her machine, I might be able to get them done faster. She's got a real good new Singer sewing machine, better than mine."

"Good idea. Keep your eyes peeled, Alice Rose. Something big is going to break in this case."

Chapter 24

SOMETHING BIG DID BREAK. In fact, things started breaking so fast, Alice Rose could hardly keep track. And then she got scared, real scared.

Two days after Carter introduced the "horse" and brought in a string of no-account witnesses who talked through their hats, Drake in his summation offered very good reasons as to why the so-called horse was a complete fabrication. The court was then adjourned, and the jury went in for deliberation.

While the jury deliberated, Alice Rose was spending her second night in a week at the home of Jewel and Horace Petty. Jewel had selected a sprigged swiss muslin and found a design in Godey's book of fashion for an afternoon tea dress. Precious was beside herself with joy. Alice Rose shared a bed with Precious, who gabbed all night long.

"This might be the best week of my life, Alice Rose," Precious said as they tucked in.

"Why's that?" Alice Rose yawned. Sharing a pillow with Precious was a lot like sharing one with a rag mop. Every night she wound her sausage curls in rags.

"Well, first of all, you being here. And Aunt Jewel just loves you and says you do the finest stitch work she's ever seen. She's going to order some of that muslin for me."

"Hmm," Alice Rose sighed sleepily. She must not fall asleep because she had to stay alert. So far, nothing big had broken and the verdict would be delivered tomorrow. She had grown to like Precious, but still she felt bad about being there. She was there to spy. "And," continued Precious, "my daddy's probably coming this week."

"Probably?" Alice Rose yawned again.

"Yes, he was supposed to come last week but decided to come this week because of the trial."

"It's almost over. Why's he interested in the trial, anyhow?" Alice Rose asked, suddenly alert.

"Well, isn't everybody?"

"I guess so," Alice Rose said. But it seemed funny that Precious's father, who had not shown up the entire time that Alice Rose had known her, should plan his visit to coincide with the trial of Eilley Orrum.

Alice Rose did not know how long she had been sleeping when she heard a knock on the back door beneath their open window, then muffled voices. Her eyes flew open. Something told her this was important. This was what all the months of Bible class had been leading up to. She was out of bed in a flash. The night was warm and moonlight flooded in through the window, lighting the back door to the kitchen. Two men stood on the stoop.

Jewel Petty opened the door.

"Judge here?"

"Well, it's about time!" hissed Jewel. "His Honor is asleep, but I'll take care of that!" She reached out and took a heavy sack from one of the men. The door was shut and Alice Rose heard Jewel Petty shuffle off to the bedroom. In a few minutes, she heard voices in the kitchen. She knew in the back hall there was a floor grate for hot air to rise through. It was right over the kitchen table where she and Precious had been cutting out the dress pattern. Alice Rose tiptoed down the hall. A kerosene lamp had been lit in the kitchen. Jewel, the judge, and a third man stood around the table. Their heads were bent so Alice Rose could not see who the third man was, except that he was tall and thin with very black hair. They were all looking down at the table, where the most enormous pile of gold coins that Alice Rose had ever seen glittered as fiercely as the sun at high noon on a summer's day.

"Well, Arthur, at last," the judge said. "All right. Here's Jewel's and my share." He raked over to one side at least half the coins and then counted them out. "Here's your share." Arthur grunted. "And the rest, you personally deliver to those jurors. Case closed. The Confederacy is richer. And when we get our percentage out of Eilley Orrum's central lead we'll be millionaires ourselves."

"I'll drink to that," the man named Arthur said.

"Let's do!" the judge exclaimed.

"Oh, I wish you wouldn't drink spirits in our house!" Jewel whined.

"Drink spirits!" Alice Rose mouthed the words. How could this lady be upset about drinking when she was about to break one of the Ten Commandments and help steal Eilley Orrum's claim out from under her, not to mention watch her husband, a judge, go against his oath of office? The judge went to fetch the bottle.

"Well, here's to our continuing success, Arthur!" With that, the men flung back their heads and downed the whiskey. Alice Rose's heart leaped in her chest. Her breath froze. The face that tipped toward the ceiling flashed with a jagged white scar as bright as lightning in a stormy night. It was Mutch's murderer. The same man she had seen in the alley behind the Bucket of Blood Saloon. And he was here in this house. Alice Rose shrank back into the shadows of the hall. She heard the judge tell him to go right away. Then she heard the door slam, and he was gone. But Alice Rose did not sleep the rest of the night. She lay like a stiffened corpse, her eyes wide open, staring at the ceiling.

The judge and Jewel Petty were quite cheerful the next morning. Alice Rose could not wait to get out of the house, but Jewel Petty insisted that first she and Precious go to Rachman's so Alice Rose could help Precious pick out fabric for a new dress. She could not keep this fantasy up much longer. She could not get through another stitch, let alone an entire dress, for the Pettys. She felt awful for Precious, but what could she say? Was it her fault that her aunt and uncle were such miserable scum-of-the-earth hypocrites? She had to see Mr. Clemens. But now here was Jewel Petty pressing a silver dollar into her hands. It was not the gold of last night, but it felt filthy to her. She could hardly touch it.

"Now that should be plenty for three more yards of muslin, and you can pick out whatever trim you want. Or if you want an eyelet apron, that would look lovely, too. Wouldn't it, Alice Rose?"

"Yes, ma'am."

They had just come out of Rachman's with their bundles when Precious squealed, "Daddy!" and began running down the boardwalk. Everything seemed to stop for Alice Rose. Her legs turned to wood. Her feet rooted in the wide plank boards. She could not move a muscle as Precious danced toward her, holding the hand of the man she had called Daddy. He approached, smiling the same narrow smile, cut by the flashing jagged scar. Alice Rose just stared. This could not be happening, but it was. He was talking to her. "Little sister," he said. Alice Rose's skin went clammy.

"She is, Daddy. She's just like my sister. She's taught me so much. How to sew and all sorts of things."

"I bet she has. What did you say your name is?" He leaned forward. The scar, which started by his eyebrow, cut down his cheek and across his mouth.

"Alice Rose Tucker," Precious said. "Her daddy is Stan Tucker and works at the newspaper."

"I have to be going, Precious. I really do. I promised my dad I'd get over to the *Enterprise* with his lunch early today." Alice Rose took off down the boardwalk. She turned the corner so she could get out of sight. Her first instinct was to run away as far as she could, all the way to San Francisco if she had to! She ducked into an alley. Leaning against the wall of a building she pressed her palms to the side of her face. She felt as if she literally had to hold her head together so she could think. She had to find Sam Clemens. That was the first thing.

Chapter 25

ALICE ROSE TURNED the town upside down looking for Clemens, but he appeared to be nowhere. The rooming house where he had lived had burned two weeks before, so he was more or less camping out with friends. She had gone to where the court would be reconvening for the verdict to be read, but none of the boys from the *Enterprise* knew where Sam was. Finally, as she was leaving, she saw him ambling down the boardwalk with Andy Drake. He was thirty feet away, but just as she was about to run to him, Precious's father stepped out from behind the courthouse building. She couldn't be seen by him. But she had to tell Sam Clemens and Andy Drake that she had witnessed a payoff last night, that the man who had killed

Mutch was back in town, and that he was Judge Petty's brother. Oh, Lord, she had never been in such a pickle.

At that moment, the Benton Line stagecoach pulled up in front of her, shielding her from Arthur Petty's view, as well as from Sam Clemens's and Andy Drake's. Alice Rose had an idea. She ran over to the stage as people were disembarking on the other side. "Hank! Hank!" she called up to the driver.

"Whatcha want, Alice Rose?"

"Shh!" Alice Rose put her finger to her lips and signaled for him to be quiet. Hank Monk looked perplexed. "Pretend I'm not here. Let me hide in the stage for a minute, then go over and fetch Mr. Clemens and Mr. Drake. Tell them it's urgent, that somebody wants to meet them in the coach. Don't say my name. Someone might hear."

Hank Monk looked utterly mystified. "Anything you say, Alice Rose."

Alice Rose crept into the stagecoach and crouched on the floor. It was several minutes before she heard the door open.

"Alice Rose!" Sam Clemens said. "What in the name—?"

"Shush! Just get in."

The two men climbed into the stagecoach.

"What's this all about?" Andy Drake asked.

"Well, first of all, you're going to lose the case. I saw the payoff last night," Alice Rose said matter-of-factly.

"So Bible class finally paid off!" Sam Clemens exclaimed. Andy Drake looked confused.

Within five minutes, Alice Rose had explained what she had seen, including the murderer of Mutch.

"Alice Rose." Sam Clemens face was creased with worry. "You listen to me. This is just too dangerous. You've been a witness to a murder and now a payoff. That's like being in quicksand over hell. You got to disappear for a while."

"Where am I going to go?"

Sam Clemens scratched his chin. "How about Chinatown, with Hop Sing?"

It was a good idea. People could disappear for days in Chinatown, even white children with gray eyes and dirty-blond hair.

Chapter 26

"THEY'RE GOING TO APPEAL, but they're not charging bribery yet. That judge is so crooked he has to screw his socks on." Sam Clemens slapped his hat down as he entered Hop Sing's shack. Alice Rose had been in Chinatown for two days. Sam Clemens had informed her father of the dangerous circumstances.

"Why don't they just come out and say he was bribed and so was the jury?"

"You want to go on record with that? Remember, your old buddy is still around town."

"Arthur Petty, still here?"

"You bet. He was seen drinking the other night with Carter at the Glory Hole. Things are starting to make a whole lot of sense, Alice Rose."

"What do you mean?" Nothing was making any sense to her right now, and Alice Rose was getting that sickening feeling she always got in the pit of her stomach when Arthur Petty's name was mentioned.

"Well, I found out it was a love match between Mutch and the preacher's wife, at least for the brief times he was sober. Her husband was an ornery son of a gun. Fire and brimstone kind of preacher. A drunk might have seemed a relief to his wife. The preacher was also thick with the Confederates and, it is thought, probably a member of the Society of Seven. In any case, the wife had quite a bit of money. A rumor got around that she had given a fair amount to Mutch, including a safety deposit key to a bank vault where some claims were kept."

"So that's why he murdered Mutch?"

"Seems so."

Alice Rose sighed deeply. "I still don't understand why Andy Drake can't just come out and say that the judge is crooked. He's got proof."

"Not proof exactly, Alice Rose."

"What do you mean? I saw him with my own eyes take that money," she said indignantly.

"That's just a tad above hearsay, Alice Rose. Well, *seesay*, anyway. The sad fact is that children aren't treated very well in this society and they are hardly ever believed. You don't have many more rights or credibility in the eyes of the law than Hop Sing here." He gestured with his arm to the shack in which they were standing. "You're a tad above a Chinaman."

Alice Rose bit her lip. She knew that, for once, Sam Clemens was not lying.

"But don't despair," Clemens continued. "Drake has one more ace up his sleeve. There is talk of a new judge in the appellate court, a good judge down in Carson City. Drake's got grounds for appeal now, he thinks."

"What's that?"

"He's being mighty cagey about it. I guess he doesn't want to tip his hand too soon. This Carter has spies out all over the place. But best I can figure is that there's one piece 'out,' as they say. A long-lost claim at the top of Eilley's, that could connect with number fifty-two. It's been out for over two years. Drake just has to check if it has been resold in the last eight months. If he can prove the claim is continuous, then he says the case would be closed. Of course, he has to find someone reliable to map it. That horse that Carter brought in maps for was a complete fabrication. You can buy anything out here from phony maps to a judge—for a price."

"I guess so," Alice Rose said quietly.

"And once he contacts the surveyors and the mapmakers, the word gets out and the other side can come in and buy them off. So he has to wait until the last minute, until he is holding his ace card."

"The scrap," Alice Rose said.

"Yes. It's the final piece of the puzzle."

"Where is this final piece of the puzzle, this scrap?"

"Somewhere at the top of the north slope of Gold Hill."

"Gold Hill, north slope."

"I believe so. He hasn't told me absolutely. He's being mighty secretive."

Alice Rose's tongue seemed glued to the roof of her mouth. This was fine. She would bite off her tongue before she told Mr. Clemens that this was the piece she and Hop Sing jointly owned. If he had thought she was in danger before, because she had witnessed a murder and a

Chapter 27

LUCKILY IT WAS SUNDAY. No one would be around, and Alice Rose knew that she and Hop Sing would have to act quickly. As soon as Hop Sing returned, she told him the news. They had agreed to meet on the north slope in one hour. Hop Sing had to go borrow some mapping and surveying equipment. They would then deliver the maps to Andy Drake personally.

Gold Hill was a mile beyond Virginia City. Not much of a walk, but Alice Rose knew she must avoid the main streets of town. So she set out across the steep scrubby terrain below E Street and Chinatown. When she arrived at Gold Hill, she followed Hop Sing's instructions to the claim near the old Belcher mine. It was late afternoon and payoff, now she really was. She might just as well be sitting bare-butt naked in a nest of rattlers. She couldn't wait until Hop Sing got home. Hop Sing could map. Hop Sing could practically see through rock. He, of all people, could tell if their claim connected with Eilley's central vein number fifty-two.

the mountain was eating the sun as fast as she could walk. She had to be careful in this terrain, for this was the site of many old and abandoned mines from the earliest excavations of the Comstock, before there were square sets and the more advanced reinforcing technology of recent years. What underground supports there were had long ago been crushed by the tremendous weight and pressure of the earth. One could easily imagine big timber supports squashed flat as pancakes and the ground caving in at the slightest footstep. Alice Rose now picked her way across an eight-acre plot of worked-out, exhausted ground. She dared not sneeze in this territory, but Hop Sing had told her that their claim was not so fragile. The timbers were still good, and soon he would have enough money to get square sets erected down through the first levels. Her shadow in the dying rays of the setting sun had become enormously long. It seemed to stretch halfway across the mountain. The abandoned headworks of old mines cast shadows like gigantic insects, monster mosquitoes, or ants frozen in the amber light of the vanishing day. Suddenly one of the shadows seemed to start an antic dance, leaping forward and overtaking her own.

"Hey!" She felt herself being picked up in the air. It all happened so quickly. One moment she was in the air and the next, she was hurtling down a dark shaft. The blackness swallowed her scream. I am dying. I am on my way to meet death. That was her only thought as the darkness of the shaft stretched before her. The end will be here soon.

But it wasn't. She had landed flat on her back. Winded, but not shattered. The impact had been oddly soft. She gradually got her breath back and in a slow inventory took stock of her body. She wiggled her foot, then a leg. It was when she began to move her arms that she became aware that she was lying on something soft and furry. Then the awful stench rolled over her. She started to gag. Turning her head to one side she saw it staring at her, shining like an even blacker moon in the darkness of the shaft. It was the eye of a sheep glazed in death. "Oh, my God!" Alice Rose said aloud. Her life had been saved by a flock of sheep. Sheep, stray oxen, mustangs, dogs, goats were always being swallowed up by shafts of old mines that had been grown over with brambles. But slowly, the realization crept up through her aching body that this shaft had not been covered. This was no accident.

Someone had tried to kill her. It came back in small pieces. The long shadow overtaking her own. The viselike grip around her chest, her feet leaving the ground. The jagged scar. Like an afterimage, the dark shaft seemed to crack with the lightning. Sheets of it crashed through the blackness and laid bare the bones of a face, a narrow, lean face. "Little sister, you've gone too far!"

The voice had followed her down the long shaft. Now it seared her ears again. She could hear it plainly, even though all was silent at the bottom of the shaft. Alice Rose began to shake. She wrapped her arms around the forelimbs and head of the dead sheep. There was another nearby. "Oh, no! Oh, no!" she whimpered. Arthur Petty had tried to kill her and she would die. She most certainly would die. For who would ever find her here? She began crying softly. She was not sure how long she had been crying when she thought she heard another noise, soft and whispery. She stopped. It was probably rats. Then there was a groan. Alice Rose opened her eyes wide. That was no animal. It was human. There was another person at the bottom of this shaft and they were hurt. Alice Rose rolled off the sheep.

A low deep cry tore the darkness. "Oh, no! Hop Sing!" He lay not a foot away from the sheep and when she had rolled off she had knocked his arm. "Hop Sing!"

"Yes." The voice was barely audible.

Alice Rose's eyes were now fully accustomed to the dark. She could see her friend's broken body lying before her. Half on his back, half on his side, his hips at an odd angle, a leg flung out behind him, his forehead caved in.

"Oh, no, Hop Sing!"

"Don't cry, Alice Rose." The words came out like small jagged pieces.

"Yes, I cry, Hop Sing. Hop Sing!" Why couldn't he have landed on the sheep? Why did her friend lay broken before her? She rocked back and forth.

"Alice Rose, I'm dying."

"No! No!"

"Alice Rose, no worry. I go to good place. I go with my ancestors. They are all waiting."

"No! You're not dying, Hop Sing. You're not." She put her hands to the side of her face and shook her head. She would do anything to put this poor broken body together. She must think of something. "Alice . . ." And with a monumental effort he said, "Rose," and his breath died, like evaporating dew on a desert flower. Hop Sing was gone.

A few minutes after Hop Sing died, Alice Rose began to go numb. Her body, her mind, entered into a shocked state. She did not feel hunger or cold, or fear or agony. It was as if her spirit had in some way already left her body. She did not know whether she woke or slept, but at one point she remembered looking at herself sleeping. It was as if she hovered somewhere above the floor of the mine. She saw the dead sheep and the broken body of Hop Sing and the form of a sleeping girl she recognized as herself, nestled between the bodies of the sheep and the man. She was not aware of any time passing. She knew she was dying and she hoped she would see her mother again and all the little babies, her lost brother and sisters that had been scattered over the western prairies and deserts. She looked forward to that time. She seemed to have long conversations with Hop Sing. He was there, telling her not to be afraid and, oddly enough, she was not. She was almost anxious now to get on with it—to simply die and see her mother and sisters and brother again.

But then she began to feel cold and discomfort. Something in her back ached fiercely and her mouth was dry and parched. Her eyes clamped shut. "No! No! Let me be!"

"She's alive! She's alive, Stan. She's alive!"

Painfully, she opened her eyes. Standing over her she saw grown men crying, grown men sobbing. Why, Mr. Clemens was collapsing into the arms of Ben Warren! And Ben Warren's face was streaked with tears.

"Joe!" someone yelled. "Stan just fainted."

Chapter 28

ALICE ROSE STOOD at the depot and watched solemnly as they loaded the coffin onto Hank Monk's stagecoach. It had been more than six months since Alice Rose's rescue and Hop Sing's death. And now this was the last good-bye. Her father, Sam Clemens, Joe Goodman, several others from the *Enterprise,* and Ben Warren, stood silently beside her with their hats in hand. Eilley Orrum had her arm around Alice Rose's shoulders. They had buried the casket in the cemetery near the graves of Alice Rose's mother and little Perry, then they had set about figuring out how to get Hop Sing's body back to China. It had taken a while but through brokers in San Francisco, Sam Clemens had made the arrangements. Hank Monk was to drive the body in its coffin over the Sierras, where it would be put aboard a ship, the *China Light,* sailing for Canton.

Eilley had paid for the whole endeavor, even though Alice Rose, now sole owner of the what had become known as the Top Spot mine of the central vein, had more than enough money. Eilley felt that she was responsible for what she referred to as "the disaster."

Alice Rose was the only dry-eyed member of the group. She understood that Hop Sing's journey would now be complete. In the long dark nights of her abandonment in the mine shaft, Alice Rose had come across a curious piece of knowledge, which was that death did not always have to be feared. She herself had been almost resentful when they had wrenched her out of the dark breast of the earth and into the sunshine again. She valued life once more, but in those few days when she had nearly died of starvation and dehydration, she had longed for death. She felt her mother so close. But it had not been time for her to complete her journey on earth.

It had taken her a while to grow accustomed to being alive again. Not only to being alive, but to being a strange kind of hero, the only kind of place like Virginia city could venerate really, aside from quick-draw gunslingers. She was rich. And not only did she get rich, but she got even. Arthur Petty and Judge Petty were now behind bars. Carter had been run out of town, and the Society of Seven left dragging its tail between its legs like the most shameful dog west of the Mississippi. Precious had been sent to her mother's in France, and it was said that Jewel Petty went plumb nuts and was living out her days with a sister who ran a saloon in Reno. There was an exquisite kind of justice in that. Spirits, not of the holy sort, all over the place. A worse fate could be imagined. Jewel Petty had gotten off fairly easily as far as Alice Rose was concerned. And she was sure that somewhere in the Bible Jewel Petty could find something to justify being a common thief, a hypocrite, and an accessory to murder.

Sam Clemens, however, had not quite pulled his last prank. Indeed, Alice Rose had nearly started to worry about him, for he had seemed awfully subdued since the disaster of last summer. But leave it to Mr. Clemens to stir something up when people were least expecting it. Although the Society of Seven had been sufficiently shamed, there were still those members who felt they had been unjustly dragged down by the crimes and despicable behavior of the Pettys. So in recent weeks, the Society had reared its unpretty head once again. There was talk about a temperance committee starting up and curfews for the saloons. It was beginning to bother Sam Clemens. He did not like to have his good times and nightly entertainments constrained in any way. When she thought back upon it, Alice Rose might have known that he was up to something.

"I would change my name entirely if I were them," Sam Clemens boomed.

"Oh, don't get all hot and bothered, Mr. Clemens. How do you spell *extract*?"

"E-x-t-r-a-c-t. What are you working on?" He and Alice Rose were the only ones at the *Territorial Enterprise* this early spring day. Sam Clemens had become most regular and punctual in his habits of late and was often the first one to work in the morning. Alice Rose had taken to writing up a few of the local items, which she found she enjoyed. "Alice Rose!" Sam Clemens said suddenly. He took his pipe out of his mouth. "What is that ball beside you there on the table?"

"A tarantula nest," she said calmly.

"What in tarnation!" He backed away from the table.

"Keep your pants on! For heaven's sake, tarantulas hardly hurt anybody out here. Besides, I got it tied shut with a piece of string."

"You do?"

"Yes, right over the lid."

"How did you get it out of the ground?"

"That's what I'm writing about. This will be an item of interest for kids. Something better for them to do than playing with old blasting caps and losing their thumbs."

"Oh, these tarantulas make nice pets?"

"For some, I guess. But if you let them out for a stroll, a wasp might get them. Wasps are their mortal enemies."

"Well, getting back to mortal enemies, I would say the Society of Seven was yours there for a while. I mean, with that claim of yours and Hop Sing's they could have knocked Eilley out of the Comstock. And they didn't care about killing the two of you in the process."

"Look, I don't like them any better than you, but they're not worth the effort."

"What effort?"

"I don't know. I have the feeling you're planning something."

"Who, me?" he said innocently. Sam Clemens took a puff on the Remains, and his entire face vanished in a cloud of smoke.

Three days later, Alice Rose burst into Sam Clemens's room at his boardinghouse. "'Who, me?'" she mimicked. "Yes, you. I should have known, Mr. Clemens, that you'd go and do a fool thing like this." She stood shaking with anger and holding a copy of that day's *Territorial Enterprise*. "It's not good enough that they killed Hop Sing, and nearly me, now you're inviting them to kill you. Huh? Is that it? You got some sort of death wish? Not good enough that we nearly had to fight the Civil War right out here on the Comstock Lode. You had to write this knowing perfectly well that half those ladies over in Carson City at the Sanitary Dress Ball are members of the Society of Seven, or at least their husbands are. And then they have to read this."

Alice Rose gave the paper a fierce shake and commenced reading: "'It has been reported that the money raised at the Sanitary Fancy Dress Ball by the ladies of Carson City has been misappropriated and sent to the Miscegenation Society.' Miscegenation! I had to look the word up—it means mixing of the races, blending of black and white people through marriage. I had to look it up, Mr. Clemens, but nobody else over the age of fourteen has to. They are talking about it all over town, in every saloon."

"That's over there in Carson City, not here, Alice Rose. Think of it this way. You increased your vocabulary."

She glared at him, "No, Mr. Clemens. They're talking about it here."

"It was supposed to be a joke. I never intended it to get in the paper. Besides, there are worse things than miscegenation, Alice Rose."

"Well, it's in the paper and it's too late now. Everybody's madder than hornets."

They remained madder than hornets, even after Sam Clemens wrote an apology. But that was not enough for some, and soon the rival newspaper in Virginia City, the

Union, jumped into the fray. Letters flew back and forth. Charges were exchanged. Clemens wound up calling the editor a liar. What had begun as a bad joke had escalated to dangerous proportions. It looked as if another battle in the War Between the States might be fought in the far-flung territory of Nevada.

Alice Rose was sitting by the window of their apartment, reading the latest of the scathing letters in the *Union,* when her father burst in. "That darned fool Mark Twain."

"Oh no, what is it now?"

"The idiot has challenged the editor of the *Union* to a duel."

"Duel? It's illegal to duel."

"Not only that. The fool can't shoot. Can't hit the broad-side of a barn. He's going to be arrested—or killed—if he doesn't get out of town fast, Steve Gillis is his second."

"When's it supposed to happen?"

"Tomorrow at sunrise, out in Six-mile Canyon."

Alice Rose was at the site of the duel in Six-mile Canyon before dawn. When she saw the tall lanky figure of Sam

Clemens accompanied by Steve Gillis, she ran out to meet them. "You have got to get out of town. You can't go through with this, Mr. Clemens." He actually looked quite pale.

"I'm in too deep, Alice Rose. I can't turn tail and run now."

"Yes, you can. Remember, you're the one who got out of the Confederate army due to the constant fatigue of retreating. Just retreat a little bit farther."

"Now listen, you calm down. Steve here is going to give me a few pointers. We'll do a little target practice."

"Mr. Clemens!"

"Don't distract me, Alice Rose."

Alice Rose walked off toward a boulder several yards away. A breeze nipped up, and the dawn rays of the rising sun shattered against Mount Davidson. It was a beautiful morning to die, she thought.

Steve Gillis had brought half a barn door for practice and set it up against a tree. He placed a squash on top. "All right, Mark, think of that as Laird's head."

"I'll try. It probably has more brains."

"Don't make jokes now, you idiot," Alice Rose muttered.

Practice commenced. The first shot rang out. Sam Clemens not only missed the squash, but the entire barn door. He reloaded. Again, he missed everything. He reloaded once more. By the fourth time, Steve Gillis was beside himself with frustration, and Alice Rose could hear Laird and his second coming up the hill through the canyon. Gillis looked as if he was about to boil over as Sam Clemens raised his gun and tried to draw a bead on the squash. If only he'd hit the barn door, Alice Rose prayed. Please, the barn door! At that moment, a mud hen flew across his line of sight and set down in the sagebrush thirty feet away. Gillis erupted in exasperation. He yanked out his old colt revolver, drew a bead on the bird, and blew its head clean off. Just as the headless body flapped to the ground, Laird and his second approached. Alice Rose silently willed Sam Clemens to turn toward the sage bush. The men saw Clemens standing there with his smoking gun and the mud hen still quivering on the ground. "What a shot, Mr. Clemens!" Alice Rose cried gleefully. "What a shot. My word, you knocked that weeny little bird's head off from fifty paces at least." She whooped and ran out from the boulder. Laird and his men stood dumbfounded.

"He hit that bird, Alice Rose?" one of the men asked.

"He certainly did. Second one this morning. Of course, three's the charm," she said, looking straight at Laird.

The duel was canceled. Laird and his men left Virginia City immediately.

But that same evening, Alice Rose went pounding up the stairs of Sam Clemens's boarding house. She carried a large bundle under her arm. She rapped on the door. Dan De Quille answered.

"Is he here?" Alice Rose asked.

"Sure is. We were about to go out and celebrate his untimely survival."

"Don't bet on it!" Alice Rose muttered. Dan De Quille began to ask why, but she shoved by him. "Mr. Clemens, now you're going to listen to me." Sam Clemens was just slipping his suspenders on, over his shoulders. "Hold it right there. You're not going to be needing those." Alice Rose nodded at the suspenders.

"What are you talking about?"

"I am talking about how there are at least five men

down at the International Hotel, all members of the
Society of Seven, who have signed up to stand in for
Laird, and are itching to blow Mark Twain's head off.
They want a duel. I am talking about a warrant for Sam
Clemens's, alias Mark Twain's, arrest has already been
issued for dueling." Alice Rose had begun to untie the
large box she had brought. "I am talking about how you
are going to climb into this dress I made for Buffalo Jo
and how I am going to tie this bonnet on your head, if I
don't strangle you first. You are going to follow me out of
here to the stage depot, where Hank Monk is waiting.
You are getting on that stage and going to San Francisco,
whether you like it or not. Because if you don't, you're
going to be leaving here in a pine box, and believe me, I
am not going to fuss about getting your bones back to
that river the way we fussed over getting Hop Sing to
China."

Sam Clemens didn't say a word. He dutifully climbed
into the dress, which fit very well, considering. Alice
Rose laced up the bodice and then tied the bonnet on.
"Keep your head down. It's dark out. We'll go down the
backstairs."

Hank Monk was waiting for them at the depot. Alice Rose picked up the back of the voluminous skirts as Sam Clemens climbed into the coach.

"Well, I guess this is it, Mr. Clemens."

"Alice Rose, hang on a minute."

"You got to get out of here."

"Look, you saved my life. I just can't skedaddle out of here that quick without a real good-bye."

"Well, you saved mine. You're the one who figured out where I had disappeared to when I was thrown down that shaft."

"That's not the point, Alice Rose."

"We both got our lives and each other to thank for them."

"Yes, so what do we do next?"

Alice Rose looked at Mr. Clemens. It seemed like such an odd question for a grown-up to be asking a child.

"I don't know."

"What are *you* going to do, Alice Rose? Go back East to the seminary and learn music and painting and drawing, maybe even Latin? You could probably buy the whole seminary now."

"Why would I want to own one? I don't know what I'm going to do. What are you going to do?"

"I'm not sure." He shook his head. "I'm sure as heck no miner."

"Yes, but you're a terrific liar. Maybe you could do it professionally, you know, write more than just lies for newspapers."

"But is it all over, Alice Rose?"

"Is *what* all over?"

He looked down at his hands, which stuck out of the sleeves, knobby and hairy. "Childhood, I guess. I think I've had one of the longest in history. I'm almost thirty now."

"Well, isn't it about time for it to end?"

"I guess so, but what will I write about? *Lie* about." He laughed.

"Write about your childhood—being a boy on that river. That's what you know best."

"Yes . . . yes," he said wearily. "I don't think I want to write about grown-up folks." He paused again and looked out from under the bonnet at her. "Alice Rose, sweet girl . . ." Alice Rose felt tears spring to her eyes. "Give me a hug, child." Alice Rose climbed into the stagecoach. Sam Clemens wrapped his long arms around her, and she buried her face in the bodice that she had so expertly pleated with over fifty tiny little crush-pleats. Curly red hair sprang out from the neckline of the dress and scratched her face. She didn't know whether to laugh or cry. "Alice Rose, I'll miss you."

"Mr. Clemens, you came along when I most needed a friend. I'll never forget you."

They said good-bye, and Alice Rose stood on the corner and watched the stage go down the mountain road and out of Virginia City, heading west toward the Sierras and eventually, San Francisco. That was the last Alice Rose Tucker ever saw of Samuel Langhorne Clemens.

Epilogue

"Alice Rose! Alice Rose, get in here quick!" Poke Williams, the telegraph operator for the *Territorial Enterprise*, called.

Alice Rose got up slowly from her desk. Her back always hurt her in the spring. It made her walk gingerly in her tall moccasins. That was the only thing that really betrayed her sixty years. That, and of course, her almost white hair. Her face was unlined and her eyes clear. She knew what she was walking toward. She had been expecting it. The comet had streaked over Mount Davidson two nights before.

She stood beside Poke now as he transcribed the taps from the telegraph. He wrote them down, and she whispered the words, "At twenty-two minutes after six, on

Thursday evening, April twenty-first, Mark Twain died at Stormfield, his home in Redding, Connecticut."

For more than forty years as editor in chief and sole proprietor of the *Territorial Enterprise*, which Alice Rose had bought with her money from the Top Spot mine, she had never missed a deadline, never been at a loss for finding the words to write a story. But now . . . What ever would she write? She watched the early shafts of light pour through the windows, and the dust motes circulating in them as in some slow dance, a sunlit quadrille. As she watched, time seemed to suspend itself. The tick of the wall clock became mute, and in between the dust motes and the still seconds, ghosts from the past slipped almost imperceptibly into the room: Eilley Orrum, Hop Sing, Ben Warren . . . and Sam Clemens himself.

She walked over to the long table and sat down at the typewriter. It was the same long table where Artemus Ward had slept, where her own father and the boys gathered around nearly a half of century before. Her hand lay still on the keys.

She remembered that other morning so many years ago, when Mr. Clemens had taken her out to see the desert bloom. She had found the snail that day and pondered its track. She thought the snail had spelled out an *M*, although Mr. Clemens had read the tracks as *O. L.*; Olivia Langdon had become his wife. Alice Rose had told him it depended on your point of view and the direction you were looking from. It all depends on your point of view, she thought. She began to type.

> Once upon a time there was an ornery little girl with dirty-blond hair and a permanent scowl etched on her face. She met a man and their first conversation took place out at the Virginia City dump. She dared him to write a story about how dag-blasted ugly the stinkhole town she lived in was. She dared him to tell the truth, that the vast, wasted desert was about as pretty as a singed cat. But he wasn't a truth teller. He was a dedicated liar—claimed he was saving up the truth to make an astonishment in heaven. We are not sure he is there by any stretch of the imagination. He refused, however, to write any of the truths the girl dared him to. Instead, he brought her to the desert one morning at dawn and dared her to look down the throat of a cactus blossom, he dared her to sit still and watch a dewdrop evaporate from a petal in the growing heat of the day.

And, Alice Rose thought, that made all the difference in the world.

Afterword

IN THE FIRST CHAPTER of *The Adventures of Huckleberry Finn*, Huck says, by way of introducing himself, that readers might have met him in *The Adventures of Tom Sawyer*. "That book was made by Mr. Mark Twain, and he told the truth mainly."

I, too, have told the truth—mainly. In certain instances, I have stretched the truth. But let me remind the reader that I set out to tell a yarn, a tale of fiction, not of fact. There are, however, plenty of facts and real people in this story. Sam Clemens, who became Mark Twain, is one of the real people. Alice Rose is not. She is a fictional creation entirely and bears no resemblance to any living person I have ever met or heard about.

Virginia City is a real place, and Sam Clemens really did live there from September 1862, when he came to work for the *Territorial Enterprise*, through May 1864, when he had to leave town in the middle of the night, in disgrace, for almost fighting a duel.

Many other characters in this book are real as well.

Dan De Quille, Joe Goodman, Steve Gillis, and Rollin Dagget all worked for the *Enterprise* and were all heavy drinkers and carousers. Artemus Ward did come to visit Virginia City, and he and the boys of the *Enterprise* did go out on a monumental binge that lasted almost a week. For the purposes of this narrative I moved Ward's visit up a year in time from 1863 to 1862.

Eilley Orrum, the Silver Queen of the Comstock, was a real person. She had come to the West as the young Scottish bride of a Mormon. Hers was one of the first really tremendous fortunes of the Comstock Lode. Eilley was, indeed, a colorful character; she needed no embellishment. She used her crystal ball, or peepstone, to guide her, and read the glistening tracks of snails for romantic instruction. Her mansion still stands overlooking Lake Washoe.

The character of Ben Warren is based loosely on Tom Peasely who was the owner of the Sazerac and the head of the Volunteer Firemen's Association. Willy Carter and Andy Drake are based on the two archrival lawyers, David Terry and William Stewart, who did engage in a heated legal battle concerning the middle lead of the

Ophir, which the Confederacy wanted to claim.

The Society of Seven is modeled after the 601 Society, a vigilante group that committed several heinous crimes in the name of Christianity in Virginia City and was mostly aligned with the Confederacy during the Civil War.

It was true that the civil rights of the Chinese were abused through discriminatory laws.

Precious Petty and her aunt and uncle are fictional creations. Judge Petty, however, bears a strong resemblance to several corrupt western judges of the era. The scene in which a payoff is delivered to his house was inspired by one I read about, in which a judge's wife gathered up the skirts of her nightgown for the men to pour the gold into, and such was the weight of the coins that her nightgown ripped and she was left standing naked in her own doorway with a heap of gold coins at her feet.

The International Hotel did not really reach the zenith of its grandeur until a few years after the period in which this story is set. The elevator was not installed until sometime later. So this is one instance where time was compressed to stretch the truth.

It is absolutely true, however, that many young boys lost their thumbs while playing with old blasting caps.

I must say a few words about words in this book, particulary those of Mark Twain. I have quoted him often, working some of his most pithy and astonishing sayings into the dialogue of this story. The first place in the narrative in which I have made extensive use of Mark Twain material is the scene where Alice Rose and he meet at the dump. Nearly all of his words about lying and religion, the Bible and Christianity, were indeed Mark Twain's own words published in his essays, his notebooks, or novels in the early part of the twentieth century. Some of these pieces were published posthumously, and some came from Mark Twain's autobiography, edited by A. B. Paine, and from Paine's own biography of Mark Twain. At this point in the time of my story, September 1862, he might not have committed these exact words to paper, but he had certainly turned over these thoughts in his head. His discourse about knowing a river so well that it eventually lost its poetry was taken from his book *Life on the Mississippi* and woven into the dialogue I created for this scene. His thoughts on what kind of hotel he would run,

I found in the book *Mark Twain's Wit and Wisdom*. The pet-rified man story was a real piece that Mark Twain wrote for the *Enterprise* and the parts quoted are verbatim.

Finally, on a more personal note, I first encountered Mark Twain many years ago as a young and voracious reader. In our backyard in Indiana there was a pond at the bottom of a hill. I built countless rafts with my best friend, and in my imagination I turned that pond into the Mississippi River. What most appealed to me about Mark Twain was that he was a person who had learned all the really important things about life and people in spite of school, church, or organized religion. Like Mark Twain it was in nature that I found spirituality. I learned about lit-erature and religion, for the most part, outside of school or synagogue.

Before writing *Alice Rose & Sam* I had written exten-sively about the old West in two other novels, *Beyond the Divid* and *The Bone Wars*, set in 1849 and 1874, respec-tively. I have also written a biography of Mark Twain, *A Brilliant Streak: The Making of Mark Twain*. One of my favorite periods in Mark Twain's life was the time he spent in the Nevada Territory and in Virginia City. I loved

Mark Twain so much I wanted to be Mark Twain; or more accurately, I wanted to be Sam Clemens. For although I had a passion for Mark Twain's books, I loved most of all the childhood, the boyhood from which the stories had grown. I had no real desire to be the famous author, but rather the wild boy. This was, of course, impossible. So I thought I would try the next best thing: to become his friend, his dear friend. To accomplish this I created Alice Rose. She is, I guess, in some sense an alter ego, although she bears no resemblance to me. But I have tried to give the two of them, Alice Rose Tucker and Samuel L. Clemens, a great adventure for perhaps very selfish reasons.

—K. L.

Cambridge, Massachusetts

January 1997